WARRIOR

Rendezvous with God – Volume Six

Bill Myers

T0355908

FIDELIS
PUBLISHING

*Discussion questions have been included
to facilitate personal and group study.*

Fidelis Publishing®
Winchester, VA • Nashville, TN
www.fidelispublishing.com

ISBN: 9781956454635
ISBN: 9781956454642 eBook

Order at www.faithfultext.com for a significant discount. Email info@ fidelispublishing.com to inquire about bulk purchase discounts.

Published in association with Amaris Media International

Cover designed by Diana Lawrence
Interior layout/typesetting by Lisa Parnell
Edited by Amanda Varian

Manufactured in the United States of America
10 9 8 7 6 5 4 3 2 1

FOR

Dale E. Brown
Brother in blood and Spirit

✍

"Being confident of this very thing
that he who began a good work in you
will perform it until the day of Christ Jesus."

— The Apostle Paul

✍

Part One

CHAPTER
ONE

WHEN WE LAST left our intrepid hero (apparently that's me), I was trying to get some sleep on a night bus out of Las Vegas. Good luck with that. It's hard sleeping when half the world hates you. Okay, maybe that's an exaggeration—just half of America. Which is understandable when you raise the wrong person from the dead on national TV.

Now I was heading east on some remote highway. I'd finally accepted the relentless pounding of the seat in front of me by some four-year-old poster child for A.D.D., not to mention the unsavory smell of his mother's egg salad sandwich. That's when the rain started. Hard. The pounding on the roof nearly drowned out the snoring of the man beside me. Our driver had to bring us to a snail's pace just to see the road until he suddenly hit the brakes sending us into a sliding stop.

"Sorry 'bout that, folks," he said through the intercom. "We've got ourselves a little flash flood up ahead."

"Flash flood?" an old woman near the front cried.

"Not to worry," he said. "Here in the desert, these things come as quickly as they—" The bus shuddered. He dropped the mic and grabbed the wheel as we started to move. Not down the road, but *across* it. He pressed the accelerator, revving hard, trying to power through it. But the water came at us too fast and too deep. People gasped, others shouted. I leaned past my sleeping companion to look out the window just in time to see us hit and sheer off a large, saguaro cactus. But that was the least of my concerns. Despite the night and driving rain, I caught a glimpse of an even darker blackness—like I'd seen in Malibu and Las Vegas.

"You might want to take care of that."

I spun around to see Yeshua standing in the aisle, leaning against a seat. The white dove that got me into so much trouble in Vegas sat perched on his shoulder.

"What!?" I demanded.

"You've become a popular fellow."

"What? With who?"

"Your adversary, the devil."

I turned back to the window. The blackness was closer; a giant, gaping maw like I'd seen in Vegas. Its edges outlined by amphibian-like faces, their own mouths open, contorted in silent screams.

Yeshua lowered his head to look out the window. "Better hurry, though. There's an impressive gorge coming up in about forty feet."

"I don't— I can't—"

"You've done this before."

"Right, but—"

"You've got the Spirit, here. Not to mention your little battalion."

"Battalion? I don't see any—"

"Trust me, they're all here."

The bus continued shaking and picking up speed; the passengers shouting and screaming.

I spun back to the window.

"Thirty feet."

"What am I supposed to do!?"

"Use your authority."

"But—"

"Twenty-five."

"Alright, alright!" I took a breath and quietly mumbled so not to be overheard, "Stop this. Whatever is going on, stop it."

"You'll have to do better than that."

"I—"

"With authority, Will. Stand."

Passengers continued crying out and yelling. My snoring companion joined in. "We're all going to die!"

"Twenty feet."

I grabbed the seat in front of me and pulled myself up. "Stop this," I repeated louder. "Stop now!"

I heard the familiar ring of steel, a sword pulled from its scabbard. Outside, I saw a blade flicker in light as it lopped off one of the dozen heads, before the sword sputtered and disappeared.

"More feeling, Will. Say it like you mean it. Raise your arms and let her fly. Twelve feet."

I raised my hands and weakly shouted, "Stop."

"Will . . ."

Embarrassed, but seeing no alternative, I went for broke. I took a breath and shouted, "In the name of Jesus Christ, I command the rain and this bus to stop! Now!"

Multiple swords appeared, flashing in brilliant bursts of light as they slashed the creatures. Could it be lightning? A thunderstorm? Thunderstorms don't shriek in agony.

The whole thing ended in seconds. The lights disappeared and the bus slowed. By the time it shuttered to a stop, we were mere feet from the precipice. There was still plenty of crying and screaming, but it came from inside the bus. The rain pounding on the roof instantly stopped. And gradually, one by one, the passengers turned to me and stared.

I awkwardly lowered my arms and took a seat, my ears hot with embarrassment. I glanced back to Yeshua and the dove. Both were gone. Now there were just the three dozen passengers silently staring. And the kid in front of me, climbing up on his seat and looking back at me.

"Cool," he chirped. "Do it again, do it again."

CHAPTER
TWO

THE DRIVER CAREFULLY worked the bus across the desert floor until we were back on the highway. There was plenty of talk and chatter over what happened, but no one felt comfortable enough to share with me—chalking it up to coincidence or figuring I was a nut job . . . or both. Only the man beside me felt inclined to speak.

"Well. Hey, now. That was somethin', weren't it?"

I nodded and was grateful he pried no further. Even more grateful that within ten minutes he was back to snoring.

Two more hours passed before we reached my stop. Well, where my stop should be.

"This is it?" I asked the driver as I stood at the open door staring into the unlit intersection. "Briarwood?"

"Just up that road, not far. Normally, I'd take you, but I don't want to risk it with the roads washed out and all. Had enough excitement for one night, wouldn't you say?"

If he only knew.

"Really ain't a town, though. Just a couple trailer homes, and a bar and rock shop."

I nodded. He said nothing more, obviously waiting for me to exit. I took my cue and stepped down onto the cracked asphalt. The doors hissed shut, perhaps a bit too quickly, and the bus pulled away, even quicker. Not that I blamed him. I'd have done the same—if I could.

With no luggage, I patted the pocket of my sports coat for the security of my cell phone and started off. The air was warm, smelling mostly of wet dirt and sand. It took forever for the sound of the bus to fade. When it did, I noticed the stillness. No hum of distant traffic. No buzz of insects. Not even a breeze. Just . . . silence. So absolute it was unnerving. The only sound was the crunching sand and gravel under my feet—so loud it made me feel like an intruder.

There were no streetlights. Not even a glow on the horizon from some distant town. But it wasn't needed. With the storm gone, a handful of clouds remained overhead—cotton balls with rims glowing in front of the hidden moon. And beyond them, stars, thousands of them. Those closest to the moon's brightness disappeared, but the others blazed with pinpoint sharpness. There was more than silence here. There was a stillness. So sublime I half-expected Yeshua to join me. The longer

I walked, the more I anticipated his presence—and the greater my disappointment.

Earlier he'd talked about something called the "Dark Night of the Soul." He said it was the final step in making men and women of faith. A time when the seed of his promises fall to earth, dead and buried. It happened to Abraham when he was about to sacrifice Isaac. Joseph when he was abandoned in prison. And Jesus on the cross. And in each and every case it was a direct response to their obedience. Not exactly the rewards program Christians are so quick to advertise. Still, after all I'd been through, I figured I was entitled to some special dispensation.

Apparently, I wasn't.

Forty minutes later, I saw a fork in the road.

"Okay," I whispered, "which way now?"

Knowing his fondness for giving last-minute instructions, I continued to approach. But when I arrived, he still hadn't answered. I slowed to a stop. "A little help would be appreciated."

No response.

"I'm trying to obey here. Just tell me which way to go."

Silence.

"Anything?" I waited. And waited some more. "A sign? A clue? Nothing big, I'll take anything."

I got nothing.

"What more do you want? I've done everything you said. Just show me. Is that too much to ask?"

Apparently, it was.

"Alright. You want me to just stay here, is that it? Just stand in the middle of the road and wait? Okay, fine, I'll do it."

And I did. For nearly an hour—until the absolute stillness began taunting me.

"Okay, fine." I turned and started down the road to my right. "If this is wrong, stop me, okay? Do whatever it takes to let me know." I kept walking. "Anything. Just tell me."

But he didn't. Was I being too impulsive? Maybe. In the past, he pointed out my binary thinking—demanding an *A* or *B* answer, when in reality the answer was oranges. I slowed then stopped. "I'm just trying to do the right thing. What do you want? Was I supposed to take the other one; is that what you wanted?" With a heavy sigh and not waiting for an answer (why bother), I traipsed the twenty yards across the rocky ground, and past who knows what hiding in the bushes, to the other road. "Is this it?"

Nothing.

"Show me!"

No clue.

No surprise.

I started walking down the road. Walking and fuming. "Alright, fine! I asked, over and over again, and you said nothing. So, I'm choosing this one. And if I'm wrong, if it leads nowhere and I wind up dying out here in the wilderness, you only have yourself to blame. Alright?"

After a few steps I slowed, giving him one last chance. "Nothing? Okay, fine!"

I resumed walking.

CHAPTER
THREE

I'M NOT SURE how long I walked down that road. Long enough for my petulance to become obvious, even to me. And embarrassing. The good news was over the months my temper tantrums seemed to come less and less frequently. Maybe I was growing up. More likely, I was just getting tired of always having to apologize when God proved himself.

God proving himself? To me? What arrogance. Why he insisted on staying with me was a mystery. And yet, it seems the only times he got angry were the times I refused to see myself as he did. "I don't make junk, Will," he said. "I would never die for garbage, so stop it with the false humility."

False humility. When he first said that, I thought he meant my humility was fake, that I pretended to be humble when I really wasn't (which was certainly true enough). But that's not what he meant at all. He was saying my humility itself was a lie. Despite what was obvious to myself and others, I was *not* a world-class loser. I was created in his image. *Imago Dei* he called it. My falseness was thinking I was some lowly, bottom-feeder instead of refusing to believe I was a child of God. Even worse, were the times I secretly felt Yeshua's dying for me wasn't enough to forgive all my failures. And, even if it was, he did so under grudging obligation. Then there was the whole business of raising me to be his "co-heir"—of actually sitting on his throne and ruling with him? The very thoughts felt like the ultimate pride and presumption. But they were his words, not mine.

Of course, when you get down to it, it really is about him, isn't it? By lifting me up, he's the one who gets the glory. Talk about a martial arts move. He takes all my failures, no matter how ugly, and flips them around to his glory. What a concept.

What a God.

I'm not sure how long I walked before it was clear I'd headed the wrong direction. I'd easily passed what the bus driver said was "just up that road, not far." Of course, I wasn't thrilled about the idea of backtracking and I let Yeshua know—already forgetting my recent repentance for grousing. (Some habits die hard.) I began turning around when I spotted a dark form hidden among giant, moonlit boulders about seventy-five yards off the road. A building? I moved to investigate.

Having no idea what desert creatures lurked behind the rocks, cacti, and whatever else was out here, I watched my every step. As I approached, a small cabin emerged amidst the boulders, one end of the roof sagging. Drawing closer, I saw it was a patchwork of weathered planks, old plywood, and rusted sheets of corrugated metal. The door was a faded red. To its left was a window with only a shard of hanging glass. There were no vehicles, no car tracks, and no footprints.

"Hello?" I shouted and was surprised at the loudness of my own voice. "Hello?" I didn't expect an answer but at the same time I didn't want to startle anyone who might be asleep—particularly if they were a lover of loaded guns. "Is anybody here?"

No answer.

I cautiously approached the door making as much noise as possible. "Anybody home? I'm a little lost out here." To my relief, I noticed a good inch of sand piled against the bottom door sill. And yet, exercising my world-famous bravery, I continued jabbering as I reached for the door to knock. "Not trying to break in or anything. Just need to—"

I was interrupted by a scream (sadly, my own) as a sudden flurry exploded over head. I ducked as a giant eagle or tiny sparrow—the distinction made little difference—flew out from under the eve and into the night. Once the attack was over, I rose, checked my pants for dampness, and knocked on the door.

Still nothing.

"Okay, I'm opening the door now." I reached to the corroded handle, a piece breaking off in my hand, and pushed. It took three more tries before the door gave way and scraped loudly across the dirt floor. The good news was there were no further attacks—though I could have done without all the quiet scamperings across the ground.

I pulled out my cell phone and turned on the light. An Airbnb this was not. In the center of the small room sat an old-fashioned, pot belly stove. To my right was a rusted bedframe complete with a tattered and stained mattress. Stacked against the back wall were wooden crates on their sides acting as shelves, probably for food and supplies—which the mice or rats or whatevers seemed to have enjoyed, with the exception of several unopened cans near the top in faded, peeling labels.

Only then did I notice the smell of coffee. Freshly brewed. I turned the light to my left. Under the window in the moonlight sat a wooden table and chair. On the table rested a very large stack of papers. Tablets. I moved to investigate, taking the four or five steps necessary to cross the room. They were legal pads—brand-new. On top was a box of unopened pencils, a magnifying glass, and a small, hand-held pencil sharpener. And beside it was a mug of coffee, its steam rising and sparkling in the moonlight. I had to smile. It seems even the "Dark

Night of the Soul" couldn't prevent his love from reaching out to me.

Behind the stack of tablets was an open Bible. Another thoughtful gesture—though considering the app on my phone, it was a bit old-school. I moved the light over to see a verse he had underlined. It was in Hosea. I leaned in to read it just as my light dimmed then flickered out, the battery dead.

CHAPTER
FOUR

I HADN'T PLANNED to sleep. But once I cleared the chair of sand and sat, sleep came hard and fast. First at the desk and, later, after finding a quilt in one of the crates, I took my chances on the stained mattress. No dreams from what I recall, just deep, heavy sleep. Not even a bathroom break which, at my age, was usually a necessity.

When morning arrived, I stood at the door watching a blazing sun spread across the landscape which, at its best, could only be described as bleak and barren. It was already hot. And I suspected it would grow worse. The smell of coffee was long gone and over the night my mouth had become bone dry. What I wouldn't give for another cup. Of anything. The moisture in the air had been sucked out, baked, and parched. Rock and sand stretched forever. The desert floor was dotted with silver-gray sage, yucca plants whose flowers had long shriveled into dead husks, and giant Joshua trees, their arms stretched toward heaven pleading for relief from the sun.

I swallowed, or at least tried, as I mulled over the underlined Bible verse I was unable to read the night before. "I will lead her into the wilderness and speak tenderly to her." I understood the "wilderness" part; hard to ignore considering the view. But "tenderly"? There was no tenderness here. And why a passage from Hosea? Wasn't that all about some prophet wooing back his whoring wife? Not exactly relevant. It made no sense, which probably meant I was smack-dab in the middle of God's will—again.

But for how long? Earlier I'd pawed through the supplies, or lack of them, searching for something. Not much there, though the number of canned peaches said there must have been a clearance sale somewhere. And no water. Surely, he didn't expect me to go without water.

I stepped from the shade of the doorway into the fiery "wilderness." As far as I could see there was no source of water—no spring, no water tank, nothing. As I said, the cabin was wedged between a towering stack of boulders, some rising forty, fifty feet into the air. Could there be something hidden among them? A spring? I wasn't crazy about the idea of searching, not because of the heat, but because of all the Westerns I'd seen as a kid—the ones featuring diamondback rattlers ready to strike. I hadn't noticed any last night but from what I hear, they only come out in the day to sun themselves.

I swore softly, or tried to—hard to swear with your tongue sticking to the roof of your mouth. I shut the door, lest some unknown desert critter decide to call the place home, and started my search. I kept mostly to the foot of the boulders, checking out the more promising crevices. I found nothing. Three and a half hours in baking heat and nothing except a soaring raven or two and animal tracks I didn't recognize. I felt the skin on my cheeks and around my eyes tightening. And what started as a small headache turned to relentless pounding. Having lived near a Washington State rainforest, I wasn't sure if that meant heat stroke, but I knew it was time to get back to the cabin.

Only when I rounded the last outcropping of rock and approached from the back side did I catch a glimpse of something brownish-red in the sun. I moved closer and saw it was a rusted hand pump, the old-fashioned kind, jutting three feet above a tiny concrete base. I arrived and gratefully grabbed the iron handle. I would have been more grateful if the heat hadn't instantly seared my hand. I unbuttoned the lower half of my shirt and pulled it up to use as a glove for insulation. I began to pump—five, six, seven times. Nothing happened. The handle moved, scraping up and down, but there was no water.

"Now what?" I whispered, not exactly angry but not exactly thrilled.

I dropped to my knees to investigate. That's when I spotted the small pile of stones and the silver reflection of water peeking out between them. I quickly pushed aside the stones to see a partially-filled, plastic bottle of water, the type you buy from any grocery store. I scooped it up and fought to unscrew the cap, cursing the flimsy plastic for twisting and bending in my hands. There wasn't much—just a few swallows. I brought it to my mouth and was about to drink when my eye caught a note resting where the bottle had sat. A faded, 3 x 5-inch index card. I hesitated, almost drank, but on second thought, reached for it. I was glad I did. Well, almost.

In large, handwritten letters it read:

FOR PRIMING PUMP, DO NOT DRINK
REMOVE CYLINDER TOP,
POUR IN WATER, PUMP
REFILL BOTTLE FOR NEXT USER

Priming the pump. I'd heard the phrase a dozen times. Is this what it meant? But that was absurd. Waste water to get water? No way. Even if it was true, a single swallow wouldn't hurt. I raised the bottle back to my mouth when I heard the voices. I turned to see I was now kneeling on a small hilltop. A small, green hilltop. I rose, a bit unsteady, to see I was surrounded by thousands of people. First-century peasants—men, women, children.

Not far away Yeshua stood among his disciples. He wore his trademark robe and sandals as the men tried to reason with him, particularly the big guy I'd come to know as Peter.

"They've been here all day," Peter was saying. "They're starving, we've got to send them home."

His companions agreed.

But Yeshua shook his head. "You give them something to eat."

"Right," Peter scoffed. "With five loaves of bread and two fish."

Another agreed. "It's some kid's lunch and we've got five thousand people here. Not to mention women and children."

"Just give them what you have," Yeshua said.

Peter shot back, "Five loaves and two fish! That's insane."

Yeshua cut him a look.

Peter glanced away, then sighed. "Alright. You heard the man." He turned back to the crowd and looked on helplessly.

One of the smaller disciples who I recognized as Matthew spoke up. "I suggest we divide them into more manageable groups."

Peter nodded. "Alright, let's get this over with."

Reluctantly, the disciples turned toward the crowd, one or two muttering, as they waded in, trying to divide and separate them.

Finally spotting me, Yeshua called, "Hey Will, how are the accommodations?"

"I've had—" I choked from the dryness in my throat. "I've had better, but—" I tried licking my lips with little success, "—I bet that's part of the plan, isn't it."

He grinned. I raised the bottle still in my hand to drink when he said, "I'd hold off on that a minute."

I looked at the bottle then reluctantly lowered it. After all, he was the Son of God.

"So, how was the coffee?" he asked.

I nodded. "Thanks."

"I still don't know what you see in that awful-tasting stuff."

"The drugs." I tried unsuccessfully to clear my throat and looked back at the water.

"You have enough paper? Those legal pads should keep you busy, right? And the pencils."

"For what?"

"You'll know." He looked back to the disciples as they continued herding the crowd. "They have no idea what's about to happen."

"Feeding the multitude?"

He nodded.

"Not great odds." I coughed again. "Two fish, five thousand people."

"And one God."

I motioned to the disciples. "Putting them in the majority."

He grinned. "That's good."

I looked back at the water.

"They're learning to trust me. Giving me all they have—even when it makes no sense."

I frowned, suspected where he might be going.

"I'll take care of the quantity, Will. Your job is to trust and give me what you have."

Now I knew where he was going.

"Remember the dad who didn't have enough faith for me to heal his son?"

I coughed and quoted, "*I do believe, help me overcome my unbelief.*"

"He gave me all he had, which for the record wasn't much, and I took care of the rest."

I stared at the bottle and began another quote, "*Give, and it will be given to you—*"

He finished, "*—pressed down, shaken together and running over.*"

"Despite the logic."

"Sort of my MO."

No argument there.

"Faith isn't about sight, Will. It's about trust. It always looks better to eat the seed than plant it. But if you trust me, you'll have an entire field for harvest." Before I could argue, pointing out my multiple failures at planting and harvesting, he added, "If you wait and know my will."

"So . . ." I held up the bottle. "You're telling me not to drink this—to pour it into the pump."

"If you drink, you'll satisfy your thirst."

"Okay . . ."

"But only for the moment."

I weighed the bottle in my hand, enjoying our conversation less every second.

"Here." He reached over and passed the basket holding the kid's lunch. "Grab something before you go."

"You'll have enough?"

He gave me a look. I shrugged and reached in.

"I'd stay away from the fish, though. It'll spoil in the heat."

I nodded and grabbed two of the loaves.

"You'll find they pair nicely with the nuts and berries."

"Nuts and berries?"

He grinned and suddenly I was back at the pump, water bottle still in hand.

It took every ounce of willpower—or maybe it was faith, I don't know—to remove the lid from the pump.

I hesitated a final moment then poured in the precious water and began to work the handle.

Nothing happened. At least for the moment. Then, after the fifth pump, I heard water gurgling up through the cylinder. Seconds later it gushed out—cool, clear, and constant.

CHAPTER

FIVE

BY THE SECOND or third day I noticed a change. Not in the scenery and not in my aching back—special thanks to the paper-thin material disguised as a mattress—but something was happening inside. Of me. As I sat in the open doorway watching the sunrise, the shadows of distant mountains slowly shifting and folding, I was again struck by the silence. But deeper than silence. Or even stillness. Like the sun, I felt it soaking into me; quieting my chattering mind, slowing those endless thoughts constantly chasing their tails. I glanced down at the open Bible on my lap. It was a verse from the Psalms. One Yeshua used earlier to explain why he occasionally left his disciples to be by himself. "Be still and know I am God."

Was this why I was here? The silence? The solitude? The—"knowing?"

I closed my eyes and for the first time heard the faint sound of chittering birds and a gentle breeze brushing across the sand. The air was sharp and clear. There was a faint fragrance of what must be sage. Earlier, everything was bleak and desolate and barren. But now, there was a growing peace. A tranquility I'd never experienced. I could sit here forever and simply—

No! I opened my eyes and sat up. Yeshua had not taken me this far just so I could go into early retirement. How many times had he said he had a plan for me, that he was preparing me (often kicking and dragging) for something? More than once he hinted I was even mentioned in the Bible. Don't get me wrong. In no way was I interested in being some spiritual superstar; my blunderings in Washington and Las Vegas proved that.

But—and this is the absolute truth—the more I got to know him, the more I wanted people to know him. The real him. Not the flannelgraph, religious icon. And definitely not the angry scorekeeper. But a God so in love with me he was tortured to death so we could be together. And no matter how much I enjoyed the peace, you can't tell others how incredible he is by sitting around examining your navel. So what was I doing here?

I rose stiffly from the chair and dragged it back into the cabin. The presence of the legal pads and box of pencils, Ticonderoga Number Two, had been sitting on the table eating away at me. I tried to ignore why they were there, but I knew the reason. More times than I could count, he asked about the books I was writing. Books, as in plural. And more times than I could count I got a few pages written then was fortunate enough to find sufficient distraction to quit. Well, there were no distractions here. I walked over to the table. Of course, I'd have appreciated a computer or even a typewriter, but if this was the best he had to offer . . .

Suddenly I was hit by a powerful wind. Roaring, hurricane style. I lunged for the table and missed, falling to the floor. I covered my head, protecting my face from flying debris and peered over to the door. But it wasn't a door. It was the mouth of a cave.

"Hang on!" a voice shouted.

I turned, squinting. Yeshua stood calmly beside me, hair blowing, robe flapping in the wind. He motioned back to the cave entrance where I could just make out the silhouette of an old man on his knees, brush and vegetation flying past the opening.

"I'm here!" the man shouted. "I'm here!"

Outside, the air was full of dirt. Rocks and boulders tumbled past. The man screamed, burying his head. And then it was over, everything strangely silent—except for the old man's weeping.

I turned to Yeshua who offered his hand for me to stand. "What . . ." I rose, taking a breath to gather my composure. "What was that about?"

"Just making a point."

I turned back to the old-timer still on his knees. "To him?"

"And you. My good friend, Elijah here, like you, has had his fair share of traumas."

"That's Elijah? You talked about him before."

"And after all he's been through, he expects me to speak with some great, melodramatic event."

"That wind?" I asked.

"But special effects are not my thing. Sure, I like an occasional sea parting or raising someone from the dead, but for the most part, my work is still and slow."

"This is for me too?" I repeated.

"Weeds grow fast, Will. Mighty oaks grow slow. And silent."

"Be still and know I'm God?"

He nodded as we watched the old man struggle to his feet. "I don't understand!" Elijah cried. "Speak to me! Speak, your servant is listening!"

Yeshua looked on with certain sadness. Then, with a heavy sigh, he said to me, "You might want to sit down."

"I'm good."

He shrugged and suddenly the ground heaved so violently I was again thrown to the floor of the cave. As it continued shaking, I pulled into a ball, covering my head from the dirt and rocks raining down.

"Yes!" Elijah screamed and began coughing. "Yes!" He was also on the ground, but with his face raised to the ceiling. "Talk to me! Talk to me!"

The earthquake stopped as quickly as it began with the last bits of dirt and dust sifting down around us.

Elijah scrambled back to his feet, still shouting, "I don't understand! What are you saying?"

Again, Yeshua helped me stand. Motioning to Elijah, he said, "He still doesn't get it, does he?"

"I'm not so sure I do." I brushed off my clothes, checking for any broken body parts. "Are you saying regardless of what happens, I'm just supposed to sit around that cabin?" He cocked his head at me. I continued, "You said we had a lot to do. It's not going to get done by stranding me in some desert."

"Hmm . . ."

"It's no use to anyone."

"Except . . ."

"Except what?"

"Except to us."

"Us?"

He crossed over to a large boulder and sat. "Tell me, Will. If I put you in a coma and you couldn't tell anyone about me, you couldn't finish writing your books, you could do nothing—would I be enough?"

I opened my mouth. He waited. But I had no answer.

"I don't understand!" Elijah resumed shouting. "Show me! Show your servant!"

Yeshua looked to him with those deep, compassionate eyes, and suddenly I felt air rushing past us. I turned to see it being sucked out of the cave to fuel a massive fire just outside.

Elijah fell back to his knees still begging. "Speak! I plead with you, speak!"

I turned to Yeshua who was looking back at me. "Would I be enough for you, Will?"

My voice thickened. "After all you've done for me . . . I'd die for you, you know that."

"Would I be enough?"

I looked down, stared hard at the ground. I had the answer but was too ashamed to speak it. He said nothing more, simply let the question sit. Eventually the fire passed, the last of the crackling and popping faded, then was gone. In the returning silence, he rose and walked toward the entrance. He kneeled to Elijah, then quietly whispered something into his ear. The old man nodded then pulled himself to his feet and slowly ambled to the mouth of the cave. Yeshua followed then, again, whispered into his ear.

"Yes," Elijah answered. "Yes . . . yes . . ."

Satisfied, Yeshua turned and walked back to me.

"He—" I cleared my throat. "He heard you?"

Yeshua nodded. "Lovers have no need to shout. Not when a whisper will do."

My throat tightened. For reasons I can't explain, my eyes began to burn. "I still don't . . . understand."

"I think you do."

I shook my head. "You talk about love and lovers. You do so much for me." I swiped at my eyes. "Why can't I do the same for you?"

"You will."

"By sitting around in some desert? I want people to know you. I want to . . ." I searched for the word. "I want to . . ."

"Exalt me?"

"Yes! Exactly. Exalt you! And not to desert snakes and scorpions but . . ."

"To the world."

"Yes!"

He smiled.

I wiped my face and was suddenly sitting in my chair at the cabin door, the open Bible still on my lap. I took an uneven breath. He may be God but he didn't understand my love. My need to "exalt" him. Yes, the desert was stunning, but sitting around enjoying some great, cosmic timeout was not the answer. I looked back to the verse, the page blurring. There it was, Psalm 46:10. "*Be still, and know that I am God.*" Wait a minute. I frowned. There was more. I blinked and looked closer. Why hadn't I seen this before? "Be still, and know that I am God," yes. But the verse didn't end there. *"Be still, and know that I am God; I will be exalted among the nations. I will be exalted in the earth."*

What? Was it possible? The command was right there in front of me, "Be still." And then there was the promise, "I will be exalted." Was there really a connection? My obedience to his promise? I closed my eyes trying to comprehend. I tilted my face to the sun, felt a hot tear slip down my face. Finally, I whispered, "I'll try." I swallowed, continued more hoarsely. "No promises, but . . . I'll try."

CHAPTER
SIX

ALTHOUGH THERE WERE moments of sublime peace, my doubts and anxiety constantly warred with and tried to overthrow them. I found it particularly difficult not knowing the time, thanks to my dead cell phone. How can you keep track of the day without knowing its progress? It left me untethered, as if I'd lost some sort of anchor. It only grew worse when losing track of hours merged into losing track of days. Not all at once, but sunrise and sunset followed sunrise and sunset until they gradually blended into each other. Was it yesterday I watched a scorpion climb out of my shoe, or was it the day before? How many events had I written on the legal pads? Did I write that one about losing my job at the university this morning or was it yesterday? And yet, losing my grip on time forced me to use a different measurement. I began sinking into moments, paying no attention to their length, only their depth.

And for the record, fasting didn't help. At least for me. At least at the beginning. The loaves of bread Yeshua offered were long gone. And those cans of peaches? Well, the ones that weren't bloated and bulging from whatever toxin was inside them, I also threw away just in case they, too, housed the same whatever toxin. And yes, the first day or so of missing food made me miserable. And, yes, I did my fair share of complaining, reminding God how trying to fast when praying over Billie-Jean, my niece's infant daughter, gave me the world's biggest headache while making me its greatest grouch. I briefly toyed with going back to the fork in the road and taking the other one supposedly leading to the town and hopefully food. But I didn't. Over the months of adventures and misadventures, I learned the importance of obedience. I didn't like it, but I learned it. And if this is where he wanted me to stay, this is where I'd stay. Fortunately, within a few days (and yes, it was days), the gnawing in my stomach and the desire for food faded. As is it did, my senses grew sharper. The sky became bluer, the air crisper. Even the green, white, and pink grains of sand became more defined.

The desert I'd originally judged as a dead wasteland continued to come alive, filled with more drama than I could have possibly imagined. Lizards sunning on stones until startled, then darting to scrubs and rock crevices. Tiny chipmunks in their white-striped masks, skittering across the hot sand in search of seeds. My trips to the water pump were often the highlight of the day. During them it was a common sight to see tarantulas crawling in and out of their holes. Once I spotted a lizard, caught in a tarantula's grip, slowly shrivel into a loose pocket of skin, the spider using its poisonous venom to liquify the lizard's insides before sucking them out. Another time I froze watching in awe as a roadrunner (which until then I suspected only existed in cartoons) snatch a rattlesnake and bang its head against a rock over and over until it was dead. Then, tilting back his own head, he swallowed the thing one inch at a time. And when he was full? He simply let it dangle from his mouth until he was ready for seconds.

And those Joshua trees? The ones whose twisted arms screamed to heaven for relief? Could it be those arms were actually raised in praise? Instead of their dead bodies strewn across the desert floor in defeat, were they simply sanctuaries for ants and beetles, offering a new version of life even in their death?

I knew I should eventually eat, but in truth, I had little interest. Not if it dulled my senses, preventing me from seeing the activity I now saw. And it wasn't just life out in the desert. Sitting here at the wooden table journaling the earlier encounters with Yeshua, I kept remembering lessons I'd long forgotten or misunderstood. Even the physical act of writing had become a type of prayer—ongoing communication between the two of us. Often, when I shook my head over some past, bone-headedness, I was certain he was there beside me, also chuckling.

My times with the Bible were no different. Without an agenda, a rush to read and finish, I would discuss passages with him. True, he remained in hiding, but deeper truths would bubble up in my mind. Impressions, unseen or discounted, some I hadn't even been able to define began making sense.

I reached for the small pencil sharpener. Inserting my pencil, I turned it round and round, sharpening its dullness into a fine point. Was this what Yeshua was doing to me? For me? Honing and sharpening? He said I had something important to accomplish. Was this really how it happened? I had my doubts but wasn't this exactly what the Father did for him? After his baptism, when God and John introduced him to the world, he didn't immediately begin his mission. Instead, the Holy Spirit took him into the desert to be tested. Was this how his own vision was fine-tuned? I remember reading, I think it was in Hebrews, where, despite his perfection, Yeshua "learned obedience"—his character being sharpened "from what he suffered."

I set the pencil sharpener back on the table and noticed how the trembling in my hands had increased. It was definitely time to get a little nourishment. But how? I had no idea. And to be honest, I wasn't that concerned. The pages, both in Scripture and what I recalled as I wrote, made it clear he would provide. "Seek first his kingdom and his righteousness," he said, "and all these things will be given to you as well." I was doing my part. And, though I still had doubts, I knew he would do his.

Outside, the light was turning orange. The sun would soon set and it would be dark. Dark, as in no light. Dark, as it would be impossible to read or write. Dark as a reoccurring and not-so-subtle reminder for me to, "Be still and know."

I was startled by the loud bang above me, followed by a series of smaller ones. Since every sound in the desert is magnified, I suspected it more to be a clattering on the roof than a bombing raid. A pebble dislodged from the rocks above me. I shrugged it off and resumed writing until it happened again. In any other time or place I would have ignored it, but here in the desert where tiny details are major events, I set down my pencil and rose. Brushing the pile of erasure shavings from my lap—Number Two Ticonderogas have no delete button—I stepped out into the parched air. Not far away, I spotted an approaching raven. I'd grown used to seeing them, just slightly larger than crows and with equally obnoxious calls. I watched it fly over the cabin then drop something from its beak that bounced along the tin roof before falling to the ground.

What on earth? I moved to investigate. On the sand lay a small pinecone. I'd seen these before, coming from trees scattered among the boulders. I stooped for a closer look. Either the raven or the fall or both split the cone open to expose tiny seeds inside. Nuts.

I heard another raven caw and turned to see it on a nearby rock. Below, at its feet, lay a similar cone. I'd often thought what Yeshua said about eating nuts and berries. But I wasn't sure which, if any, were safe or poisonous. The second raven hoped to the ground and pecked at the cone until it pulled out a tiny nut and nibbled away.

I had my answer. One I'd not have found if I hadn't grown silent enough to hear the desert. But it was more than just hearing. As I said, something else was happening, deeper. A type of cleansing. Detoxification. It was impossible to define, until much later, well into autumn, when I had the dream.

CHAPTER

SEVEN

YESHUA WAS TRUE to his word when he said he would be silent during my Dark Night of the Soul. But, as I've pointed out, being the creative type, he found plenty of other ways to communicate.

Desert . . . check.

Solitude . . . check.

Fasting . . . check.

Scripture . . . check.

Journaling . . . check.

And there was still another area I'd not planned on. I found it in Acts 2:17. "In the last days, God says, I will pour out my Spirit on all people. Your sons and daughters will prophesy, your young men will see visions, your old men will dream dreams." By my morning stiffness and middle-of-the-night bathroom breaks, I obviously qualified for the later.

Weeks continued to pass. Don't ask me how many. Like I said I'd quit counting. But it turned cold, bitterly cold. Initially, when I saw the magnifying glass that first night, I hadn't understood, much less appreciated it. But now, thanks to the absence of central heating and abundance of dry, desert wood, I got the memo. I was no survivalist, but it didn't take long to use the scraps of wood, magnifying glass, and sunlight to stop from freezing.

In any case, I was sleeping soundly when I felt something on my chest. I opened my eyes to see the dove sitting there, preening himself.

"Uh . . . you're back," I said.

He cocked his head at me over the obvious, then fluttered across the room and out the door—the door I clearly shut before going to bed. That was my first clue it was a dream. My second came when I threw back the covers to discover I was wearing a rented tuxedo and dress shoes.

I pulled myself from the bed and stepped outside into an area I had never seen. The stars were the same, sharp and clear, illuminating the desert with pristine light. But the Joshua trees I named surrounding the cabin (like I said, I had plenty of time) and the rest of the terrain were entirely different. Nothing was familiar, particularly the stone monument that rose from the desert floor and loomed a good four stories over my head. It appeared to be the back of some giant throne with a statue of a man sitting on it. From where I stood I had no idea who he was. I did, however, recognize the other man—the one on his knees groveling before the throne.

"That's . . . that's me," I gasped. I turned to the monument. Even from the backside I knew, I sensed it had nothing to do with God. And yet, there I was, face planted in the sand, my hands outstretched in obvious worship.

"No." I shook my head and turned to the dove perched on a nearby rock. "I wouldn't do that. No way would I worship anyone but God! Why would I do that?"

The dove sat silently.

I frowned, trying to process. Then I approached the man, the mock replica of myself, ready to expose the counterfeit. He wore the same clothes, had the same shaggy hair, and the same scruffy beard, whose prickling itch I'd finally grown accustomed to.

"Get up," I ordered. "Get up!"

But he remained bowing.

"Get up!"

Still no response. Apparently, I was as stubborn in my dreams as I was in real life.

I turned back to the monument. Slowly, cautiously, I worked my way around to the front. As I moved, I began to hear swearing—not the vilest of oaths, but enough. More unnerving was the fact they were identical to the words I use when I'm angry. And when I finally arrived at the front, I saw the source. The figure on the throne was a statue of me! The angry me. Its moving mouth and lips responsible for the cursing.

I looked on, stunned, until the message slowly dawned. At least I thought it was the message. All this time I figured my language was a small infraction, particularly given our culture's casual use of it. And I always planned to clean it up, eventually. By the looks of things, "eventually" had finally come.

"Alright," I called. "I'll work on it. You have my promise." But the statue's oaths only grew louder. "Yes!" I repeated. "I understand. I get it!"

But I didn't get it. Not until the servants suddenly appeared. Dozens of them, racing back and forth to my statue carrying bowls of fruit, drinks on trays, platters of bread, cheese, and wine—all my favorites. But the servants weren't moving fast enough, at least for my statue, which explains its anger—which explains its language— all directed at the servants not fulfilling its wishes.

But the servants weren't vague, nondescript entities. I could have lived with that. Instead, as I looked closer, I saw they were the same person. The same person multiplied a dozen times. Each and every one of them Yeshua!

My jaw slacked. "No!" I spun around searching for the dove who now sat atop a prickly pear. "I . . . I would never say that! I would never say those things, not to him!"

The dove gave his head a shake, ruffling his feathers.

I turned back to the scene—the swearing, the racing servants. Was it possible? I scowled, pushing away the thought but it kept returning. I was swearing because I was angry at the circumstances. But—and this was the punch to my gut—I was swearing at who was responsible for the circumstances. And it wasn't the oaths; they were superficial, a symptom of something deeper. Because underneath was the real issue. Underneath was my anger at the One ultimately in charge.

I could barely finish the thought. How was that possible? I had given him my life. I chose to serve him. Me serving him. And yet, the cold truth before me was my anger at God. I was swearing at God for not serving me! It exposed an internal poison I would never have imagined but could no longer deny. I felt my legs weaken. I might have fallen to my knees like the other me—the one so busy worshipping me—if it weren't for the dove. I heard his wings whistle softly as he rose from the cactus. I watched as he approached, hovering just a few feet ahead, making it clear I was to follow.

CHAPTER
EIGHT

WE CROSSED TO the other side of the statue, where the stone legs met the sand. And between those legs, lost in the shadows, was a passageway. From inside came the sound of knocking. Continual. The dove fluttered in, but I waited. When he didn't fly back out, I took a breath, reminded myself it was only a dream, and followed. In the dim, flickering light, the passageway stretched on forever. Along both walls were hundreds of large, iron doors, every one open. Except for the one closest to me.

And the source of the knocking? Yeshua. He stood at the door, patient and persistent, rapping away.

"You sure get around," I said.

Without a word, he stopped knocking and stepped back, motioning for me to give it a try. I first tested the door by giving it a push. I was surprised at how easily it swung open. Why he hadn't tried that was beyond me. When I turned back to ask, he was gone.

So was the dove.

But not me. In more ways than one. As with the multiple images of Yeshua outside, there were now multiple images of me inside. Actually, just three which, trust me, were enough. I cautiously stepped through the door and it immediately slammed shut behind me. I spun around but there was still no sign of Yeshua—except for the knocking that resumed on the other side.

I turned back to the room. It was the size of a small gymnasium and bathed in bright, blue light. To my left was the first me; sitting atop a mountain of books, fifteen, twenty feet high—novels, biographies, fiction, you name it. How I loved books—reading them, feeling their texture in my hands, breathing the smell of paper and ink. And, now up on the pile, I was reading many of my favorites: Dante, Dickens, Shakespeare, Donne. But something wasn't right. I watched as I finished one book and tossed it aside to reach for another. Quickly scanning it, I reached for another. After that, I reached for yet another. And then another. And another. I was furiously reading, desperate to get to the next. And the next and the next—devouring them like a man starving to death. But I never seemed to be satisfied. My hunger always growing.

The knocking on the door continued. Steady and relentless.

I turned to the second me. The one who stood across the room dressed in my usual sports coat and tie. I was lecturing twenty or so students. "Besides Chaucer and Spencer," I said, "who made iambic pentameter so accessible and famous?"

The kids eagerly took notes and not just because my tests were tough. Well, alright they were that. But teaching was my joy. What I was trained for. What I thrived on.

"What playwright?" I repeated.

"Shakespeare," a student called out.

"That's right!" I shouted. "That's right!"

But, just as in reading my mountain of books, something wasn't right. As I lectured, I paced, relentlessly calling on students, correcting them, pressing them faster, harder, louder. "And why is this rhythm so popular?" No one answered. But I was driven to impact them, I had to influence them. "The heartbeat!" I shouted. "da DUM da DUM da DUM. Iambic pentameter! It's the human heartbeat, people! How many times must we cover this? The human heartbeat!"

They nodded, they wrote, but it wasn't enough. As with my books, I needed more. I needed them to satisfy some hunger, to quench some unquenchable thirst.

And still the knocking continued.

I turned back to the door. But there was one more of me to witness—the one at the far end, sitting at my dining room table back home. We were at another one of Darlene's Sunday, Southern spreads—fried chicken, mashed potatoes and gravy, cornbread, collard greens, the list went on. And we were all there:

Fifteen-year-old Amber sharing her schizophrenic logic: "If it didn't make sense, I'd understand it!"

Beautiful Patricia, the fundamentalist: "Some of our top scientists believe in creation."

Darlene, her liberal, arch nemesis: "Before or after they fell off the edge of the earth?"

Billie-Jean, sitting in her highchair exploring new ways to wear mashed potatoes.

And Chip, Amber's boyfriend who seldom missed a free meal or the opportunity to enlighten us with his expertise on everything.

Yes sir, good times had by all—at least as I looked back at them. And yet, watching my third self sit at the table, enduring my dysfunctional "family" in silence (I quit trying to get a word in long ago), I knew something vital was missing. Like my books, like my teaching, there was an emptiness. I thought of Yeshua's metaphor back when we first met—the difference between the empty balloon and the filled one.

I'd seen enough. I turned to the knocking at the door, crossed to it, and flung it open. I was startled at the sound of fluttering wings and the cold, morning light striking my face. I opened my eyes to bright sunlight streaming in through the cabin's open doorway. I took a breath and blew it out. Then another. It was a dream, only a dream. But it held plenty to unpack.

And here, alone in the desert, I'd have plenty of time.

CHAPTER
NINE

AND SO THE purging continued through the winter. Several times I thought about counting the days—like marks on the wall by a prisoner in solitary confinement. But this was no punishment, I knew that. And I was no prisoner. I could call it quits any time I wanted. And believe me I wanted, more than once. But there was still that compassion for him and my longing to express it. Even at that, I knew the longing was actually his. He's the one who started it. He was the author. I was merely the recipient wanting to return it. Receiving and giving. Giving and receiving. A perpetual cycle of . . . well, there was no other word for it but love.

But none of it came fast.

I remember one moonless night, laying on a high, flat rock looking up at the stars. Over the past several weeks the sky had grown much hazier, although I could still just make out my favorite constellation, I think they call it the Seven Sisters. Even as a kid up in Washington, I staked it out as my own. As I stared, trying to count all seven, a shooting star flared by overhead, very close. It was silent and spectacular. Then, as suddenly as it appeared, it was gone as if it never occurred.

I thought of this for a long time—how it was there one moment, dazzling in glory, and then forgotten. The other stars remained stable, night after night, generation after generation. As spectacular as it was, no sailor would guide his ship by the fleeting splendor of a shooting star. If I wanted to serve, to share his inexpressible love, which would I rather be?

Despite my whining and complaining—and, yes, I had plenty of time for both—it was no contest. I'd wait here as long as it took to prepare me. He once said he was more concerned about who I was than what I did. I wasn't fond of the idea. Still, if he wanted some gnarly old tree, growing inch by imperceptible inch, instead of a young flower whose beauty sprouted quickly then faded in a season, so be it.

But trees grow best in groves and forests where they can protect one another from the wind and storms of life. And, as much as I enjoyed the solitude (when I wasn't complaining about it), I wasn't prepared for the next step . . .

∽

Over the months I'd become accustomed to peace and the lack of human drama—particularly when it came to crying babies and screaming teens (or is it screaming babies and crying teens?). Either way, I enjoyed the stillness while at the same time slowly sipping the Scriptures and slogging through my daily writing. But I wasn't in complete solitude. Besides tarantulas, scorpions, and snakes, I had larger friends including rabbits, chipmunks, and a bobcat whose tracks were fresh every morning, but who I saw only once atop the boulders, his eyes glowing like Smeagol from *Lord of the Rings*. I even enjoyed the night yappings of a small family of coyotes and the hootings of a pair of star-crossed owls.

When it came to dining pleasures, I could do without the steady diet of pine nuts (although it proved to be a great weight-loss program). But by watching what the birds and other animals ate, I slowly and cautiously expanded my menu. For the record, prickly pear cacti are not as tasty as you may think, and by no means try a Joshua tree.

The days grew warmer and longer. As best I could tell, summer was on its way. And for reasons I didn't understand, the sky grew even more hazy. I was half a mile from the cabin, warming myself on an outcropping of boulders and reading one of my least favorite Bible passages by James, Yeshua's half-brother:

> "Consider it pure joy, my brothers and sisters, whenever you face trials of many kinds,

because you know that the testing of your faith
produces perseverance. Let perseverance finish
its work so that you may be mature and complete, not lacking anything."

Seriously? Christians were being tortured and mur-
dered, some used as human torches to light Roman patio
parties, and James had the gall to write them this? Sure,
life could be hard—ask the guy who recently took up
desert living—and, yes, I understood the concept of
becoming "mature and complete, not lacking anything."
But this? And for those poor, first-century Christians?
Where would it end, all this suffering?

I was just pointing this out to Yeshua when I noticed
a large, brown cloud in the distance. Any rain or snow
would be appreciated. I'd seen neither since that night
on the bus over half a year ago. But rain and snow are
not accompanied by a giant cloud billowing across the
desert floor.

They call them haboobs. Dust storms. I read about
them but never saw one, at least in person. It was breath-
taking, rising at least a thousand feet into the sky, dense,
brown, and pluming forward as if in slow motion.
Magnificent.

It would have been more magnificent if it wasn't
headed toward me. Still, at that distance, ten or fifteen miles, I saw no problem. I could easily run to the

cabin for shelter. I'd even have time to double-check the window I'd covered with cardboard ripped from the back of my legal pads. Ingenious, right? Robinson Crusoe would be proud.

He would have been prouder if, after rising and exercising my athletic prowess by hopping from boulder to boulder, my foot hadn't slipped into a crevice. (Apparently my athletic prowess isn't what it used to be.) I immediately felt the pain of a sprained or broken ankle. Sadly, that was nothing compared to the grumpy rattler I disturbed—the one who welcomed my intrusion by sinking his fangs deep into my ankle. Painful? Think bee sting times two.

I yanked my foot out but not before he struck again. Think beehive. I grabbed my ankle and rolled away—right off the boulder, a good eight feet to the desert floor and, full disclosure here, broke my moratorium on using bad language.

I kicked off my shoe and peeled away my sock. The puncture wounds were clearly visible, all four of them, and already turning red. After a little more swearing—what did Martin Luther say, "if you sin, sin boldly"?—I turned back to the dust storm. It was several miles away but rapidly approaching. I tried standing and fell. I tried again. And fell again. I resigned myself to crawling, searching for a stick to use as a crutch. There was nothing. Except, twenty maybe thirty yards away, I spotted a pinon pine. If I could reach it, I'd break off a branch and use it.

I tried one more time to stand and to hop, but the tree was too far away and I fell back to crawling. Besides the searing pain in my ankle, I felt a tingling like pins and needles in my calf. The venom was doing its job. I finally reached the tree and pulled myself up the rough, furrowed trunk. There was a branch, but just out of reach. I lunged for it and fell. I looked at the storm. It was closing in. I crawled back to the trunk and worked my way up. I felt nauseous. My head pounded. Using both feet, I cried out in pain as I leaped for the branch. This time we connected. I held on. It bent under my weight but was too green to snap. I bounced and swung. It cracked but would not break. Unable to hang on (we've already discussed my athletic prowess), my hands slipped and I fell back to the ground.

I looked over to the wall of boulders. There was no need to check on the sandstorm, I heard it coming, low and rumbling like a freight train. No way I could make it back to the cabin. Not like this. I resumed crawling, this time toward the wall. Gusts of wind picked up, throwing spitz and sprinkles of sand. I felt my head growing light. The rumble grew to a roar. Wind blew, tugging at my shirt and hair, blowing sand into my eyes and nose and mouth.

I arrived at a smaller group of rocks spilling from the wall. Suddenly, I retched. I stopped crawling and retched again. Wiping my mouth, I raised my head, searching the wall still some ten feet away. The wind began whistling. It grew harder to think. But there had to be some protection there, some mini cave I'd even be willing to share with a dozing rattler.

More retching; this time green bile. I resumed crawling. Sand burned my eyes making it impossible to see as the wind howled through the rocks. The wall lay just ahead. I caught a glimpse of a ledge jutting out—three, four feet high and about that long. Below it, a black opening. Crawling more on autopilot, my head spinning, unable to think, I pulled myself toward the darkness until I felt the coolness of shade. I dragged myself another foot, maybe two, before I hit the back wall and collapsed.

CHAPTER
TEN

"CONGRATULATIONS."

It was night when I pried open my sand-crusted eyes. Yeshua sat on the ground leaning against the outside of my "cave." I tried sitting up and winced at the pain in my head, then my leg, then anywhere else you can imagine.

"Right," Yeshua said. "I wouldn't try that just yet."

I eased back down and noticed how hard I was shivering. "I'm still here?" I asked.

"Not for long." He looked up at the sky. "I'm sure missing the stars, aren't you?"

"Not for long?" I repeated. "Does that mean I finished? I passed this Dark Night of the Soul course?"

He turned to me.

"Yes?" I asked again, allowing myself to shiver for some sympathy.

"It's not a course, Will. I'm not something to pass."

"Then . . . ?"

"Think of this as a pause button—allowing the knowledge in your head to filter down into your heart." I scowled and he replied, "It takes time for your flesh to become my life."

"But it's happened, right? I'm through here?"

"You've laid a great foundation. I couldn't be prouder of you. There'll be refresher times, of course. But yes, you're through."

I fought to sit up again and vomited. Wiping my mouth, I swore—or thought about it. Either way, he heard.

"Sorry," I muttered "still working on that."

He smiled. "It's not the language, it's the anger."

"I'm not mad at you. It's all this, this—it's everything that's been happening."

It was a lame argument and we both knew it. But he let it slide. Instead, looking back to the sky, he clasped his hands behind his head and quoted, "*Consider it pure joy, my brothers—*"

"Okay," I interrupted, "I get that hard times are supposed to be like some sort of faith workout. But some of this seems so . . . so . . ."

"Pointless?"

I dodged the obvious by moving and tossing in some overly dramatic wincing. But he knew all the tricks. Instead, he quoted another passage. "*In all things God works for the good of those who love him—*"

"Yes, I know, I know," I said. "That's Paul, what he wrote in Romans."

"Very good. And here's another one of his favorites . . ." He waited for my attention before quoting, *"Rejoice always, pray continually, give thanks in all circumstances; for this is God's will for you in Christ Jesus."*

I blew out a breath of frustration and, yes, anger. "That's easy for him to say. He's not been out here all this time, going through all this, this—"

Suddenly we were in a darkened room, its walls made of limestone blocks. Morning light filtered through a small, circular opening in the ceiling. On the stone floor, a bald man in his late sixties, slept on a thin, straw mat. Once I got my bearings, I turned to Yeshua who was still beside me.

He nodded, answering my question. "Paul. The morning of his execution."

I looked back to the old man, feeling both awe and pity. This was the great apostle Paul. And yet . . . look at him.

Yeshua continued, "May I quote to you what he wrote to some folks in Corinth?"

I nodded. He closed his eyes and softly recited, *"Five times I received from the Jews the forty lashes minus one. Three times I was beaten with rods, once I was pelted with stones, three times I was shipwrecked, I spent a night and a day in the open sea."*

I listened, marveling at the saint who slept before us.

Yeshua continued, *"I have been constantly on the move. I have been in danger from rivers, in danger from bandits, in danger from my fellow Jews, in danger from Gentiles; in danger in the city, in danger in the country, in danger at sea; and in danger from false believers. I have labored and toiled and have often gone without sleep; I have known hunger and thirst and have often gone without food; I have been cold and naked."* Yeshua came to a stop, letting the full meaning sink in and take hold.

I slowly nodded and repeated, *"Rejoice always."*

"Yes," Yeshua said.

"In all things God works for the good of those who love him."

"Yes."

"Give thanks in all circumstances."

"Yes. Not *for* all circumstances, but in the midst of them."

I motioned to the apostle. "And this is how it all ends?" Yeshua remained silent and I pressed in. "What good did it do him? He's lying here, all alone, forgotten in some cell—and now he's about to be killed?"

"For the next two thousand years his words will change the world."

My throat tightened. "But . . . he doesn't know that; he doesn't know the future."

"And neither do you."

"What are you saying? I'm not . . . I'm no Paul."

"You, along with all my brothers and sisters, have the same power, the same Spirit inside you." I swallowed, looking on. "More importantly, Will, you have the same love."

I was startled by headlights washing across the room—a novelty for first-century jail cells. I shielded my eyes and realized I was back in my mini cave. Yeshua was nowhere to be found. The car, I guessed a pickup, bounced to a stop. Doors opened and slammed. I watched two silhouettes approach—an old man in a cowboy hat and some heavyset woman in flamboyant gray hair that glowed in the headlights. With effort they stooped down to examine something in the sand.

I tried to shout, "Here . . ." but my throat was like broken glass.

"Looks like the shoe," the cowboy said.

The woman agreed. "From the dream."

"Here . . ." I croaked. "Help . . ."

"Listen," she said. "Over, against those rocks."

A flashlight appeared, sweeping in my direction.

"Here!" I coughed. "Here!"

The light flared in my eyes. They rose and started toward me. The cowboy was the first to arrive. "You alright?" He knelt and began dragging the sand away from my opening.

The woman joined us; her voice hoarse as if cured in decades of smoke. "What're doing out here?"

"Long story," I choked. "You wouldn't . . . believe it."

"Can't be no stranger than ours," Cowboy said. "What's wrong with that leg? Looks terrible."

"Snake bite," the woman said. "From Chip's dream. Remember? I told you the kid had a gift."

PART TWO

ELEVEN

IF YOU THOUGHT Chip's presence was more than coincidence, you'd be right. He tracked my cell phone before it died and eventually hitch-hiked to wherever we were. If you thought his presence had grown less irritating during my stay in the desert, you've overestimated his maturity—or mine.

"You had a dream?" I asked as I hobbled alongside him across what Briarwood called a street.

"Oh, yeah, dude. My powers are way more awesome than in Malibu when we kicked all those demon butts." There was only the slightest whiff of truth in his bluster, but experience said it would do little good to correct him—not that he'd give me the chance. "But it was the post someone made on that bus when you called down God's wrath that really got my attention. Me and lots of other people."

"God's wrath?"

"You know, the drought."

"Drought?"

"And raising that dude from the dead in Vegas."

"You saw that?"

"Hard to miss on national TV. Course you got the wrong guy, him being a killer and all, but everyone makes mistakes, right?"

I was finding it difficult to breathe, and it wasn't the fading effects of the snake bite. Regarding the bite . . . It took nearly seventy-two hours of drifting in and out of consciousness before I was strong enough to begin walking. Now, at 4:50 in the afternoon we approached a small, weathered building. Once we arrived, Chip pulled open the door and we entered the back room of Briarwood's Rock 'n' Gem Shop.

As my eyes adjusted, I saw four of the town's finest citizens (I'd soon learn its only citizens) sitting in folding chairs around a scarred and stained, oak table. The first two I recognized—Cowboy—a.k.a. Gustoff Rutherford—owner of the rock shop. His arms and face were blackened from years of desert living. The second was Sophia, the woman in the flyaway hair. She was currently clad in a bright shower curtain of a dress. She owned the small café/bar/New Age gift shop with a tiny office in back where I'd been recuperating—and where she helped in my recovery with a foul-smelling concoction of plants, herbs, and ingredients I was too afraid to ask—though I suspect a sizeable portion involved whisky.

"Dr. Thomas," Cowboy grinned, his teeth yellow but still intact. "Please sit, sit." I pulled up a chair and Chip joined us. "So, how you feelin'?"

I nodded and tried to smile. "A lot better, thanks to the both of you."

"And my Chakra Charm." Sophia gave a husky laugh which turned to a fit of coughing. After recovering, she added, "A little kick to pull you through, right, Doc?"

I tried another smile.

"In any case," Cowboy cleared his throat in disapproval, "We just wanna say how honored we are that you chose to be with us."

I frowned. *Chose* wasn't exactly the word I'd have picked.

"And you're welcome to stay as long as you want," Sophia said.

A second woman beside her spoke. She was blonde, slender, and in her forties. She wore white shorts, a pink polo shirt, and a tennis bracelet that sparkled in sunlight from the room's only window. "And should Sophia's accommodations not meet your needs, my husband and I would be more than happy to offer our home."

"Kinda like a mansion," Chip said. "They got a pool and everything."

"Thank you, uh . . ."

She smiled. "Victoria."

Sophia coughed then cautioned, "Not Vickie, but Victoria."

Cowboy added, "Her husband ain't no believer."

Victoria smiled. "Not yet."

"But he's sympathetic to our cause," Cowboy said.

"Cause?" I asked.

"To spread the gospel, of course."

"Right." I nodded. "Of course."

He continued, "We been prayin' to beat the band. And now you suddenly showin' up—well that's no accident, right?"

Sophia agreed. "Cosmic convergence."

Note to self: Plan another talk with Yeshua.

"With your fame and such, no tellin' how fast we'll be growin'," Cowboy said.

Sophia nodded. "But you should know you're winning no fans with that curse of yours."

"Curse?" I asked.

Cowboy added, "Even had some Feds sniffin' round way back when you first disappeared. But if that's what it takes to get an ungodly nation to pay attention, so be it."

"Um . . ." Unsure where the conversation was going, I looked to the fourth member of the group—a frightened wisp of a girl, early twenties with more ink tatted on her arms and neck than the *Seattle Times*. "And you are?"

"Oh, that's Fern," Cowboy said. "She's just passin' through."

Sophia reached over and gave her hand a squeeze. "But she's welcome to stay as long as she wants."

Victoria explained, "She had a little falling out with her boyfriend."

"You mean pimp," Cowboy corrected.

"Rutherford," Sophia scolded.

"Jes callin' it like it is." Fern examined the table as Cowboy continued, "God's all 'bout truth. And if this man's gonna be our pastor he needs to know the—"

"Excuse me?" I said.

Sophia shrugged. "Pastor, spiritual advisor, whatever you call yourself."

"To look after our little church," Cowboy said.

I swallowed. "Church?"

Cowboy quoted, *"For where two or three are gathered together in my name, there am I in the midst of them.* Matthew 18:20."

Before I could respond (with what I wasn't sure), I heard crunching gravel from a car approaching outside.

Cowboy pulled himself from his chair to look out the window. "They're here."

"They?" I asked.

He limped toward the door. "Your friends."

I turned to Chip who explained. "After the rescue, I made a couple calls." He rose and followed Cowboy who had opened the door.

In the bright sunlight I watched a red, dust-coated SUV pull to a stop. Chip squeezed past Cowboy to step outside. The front passenger door opened and a girl stepped from it, shading her eyes from the sun.

Chip shouted, "Amber!" and started for her. "Ambrosia!"

Spotting him, she cried, "Chip!" She ran toward him as the driver's door opened and Darlene Pratford stepped out. She stretched, surveyed the landscape with an oath, then opened the back door to retrieve Billie-Jean from her car seat.

Yes, Yeshua and I definitely needed to talk.

CHAPTER
TWELVE

THAT FIRST AFTERNOON turned to evening as everybody settled in—for how long was anyone's guess. Darlene, Amber, and Billie-Jean joined Chip at Victoria's palatial sunbird home. I chose to stay on Sophia's backroom cot—not because I was averse to luxury, swimming pools, and Jacuzzis, but because Victoria only had two extra rooms and I had no desire to become Chip's roomie nor he a desire to trade places and sleep on my cot. Sophia had her own doublewide next to her store. Fern stayed in a small pickup camper on the other side, while Cowboy lived in a cabin a hundred yards down the "road." Two other trailers with no occupants and plenty of rust lay further out. Welcome to Briarwood, Utah, whose population had just doubled.

I'd worn myself out—returning to the land of the living was more exhausting than I expected—but knew I should accept Cowboy's invitation for coffee and some debriefing in the back of his shop. Other than a quiet, muffled rattling from the next room, the place had a peaceful, Old West kind of vibe. Two deer heads mounted on the wall. A stuffed bobcat on the counter, along with three stuffed quail. I wasn't going to ask where he got the buffalo head.

"Yes sir," he said as he set a turquoise mug, straight from a 1950s diner, on the table before me. "I'd say just 'bout everyone in the country knows you by now. Course not everyone believes it's your doin', the drought, I mean." He poured me an oil-thick cup of coffee from a glass carafe clouded by years of use. "Got the usual nonbelievers. But they'll come around. Give 'em time."

He poured his own cup, then dragged a chair across the scarred, pine flooring. He removed his cowboy hat and sat facing me for what I suspected to be an Old West, man-to-man conversation. I chose not to ask if he had French vanilla creamer.

"You doin' good?" he asked.

"Oh, yeah." Truth is I still felt like I'd been hit by a semi.

"Snake bites can be troublesome."

"For some. Yeah, I suppose."

He leaned back in his chair and took a sip of coffee. I stared at my own knowing I'd eventually have to do the same. But first things first. "You said," I cleared my throat, "you said government officials were here?"

"Sniffin' round like dogs on a hunt." He took another sip. "What you done with that kid tryin' to kill the California governor definitely got their attention. The fact he's runnin' for president, don't hurt."

"Governor Proctor made the announcement, then?" I manned up and sipped the coffee, barely making a face.

"And with the wife of your preacher friend gettin' killed protectin' him." He took a breath and continued, "Folks say he'd make the perfect running mate."

I choked. "I'm sorry, do you mean Trevor Hunter?"

Current president ain't shy endorsin' them, which is fine by me. It'll be good to have a couple real Christians in the White House."

I closed my eyes, remembering all too well the dark presence Chip and I saw around Governor Proctor's limo . . . and Trevor Hunter's headquarters.

"You okay?"

"Yeah, it's just," I cleared my throat again, "things aren't always as they appear."

"Like you raising that killer from the dead?" Before I could respond, he quoted, "*For as the heavens are higher than the earth, so are my ways higher than your ways, and my thoughts than your thoughts.* Isaiah 55:9."

I blew out a breath. He got that right.

"But here you are, come into our presence just like your protégé dreamed."

"My protégé? You mean Chip?"

"Elijah's little Elisha." He chuckled. "A bit green but I guess that's how it is with prophets in training, heh?"

I set down my mug. "Listen, I think you've overestimated me . . . and Chip. I mean this whole pastor thing, it's really not something I'm cut out for."

"Yup."

"Yup?"

"Humility: A sure sign of a Lord's righteous servant. But you're forgettin' our prayers."

"Prayers?"

"Been prayin' for a preacher well over a year, now."

"Right. Well, I appreciate your prayers, but I'm no leader."

"Exactly what Saul said in First Samuel, chapter nine.

"It's not what I—"

"We seen your miracles not just on the bus but in Vegas and up in Washington too. Just like Nicodemus said back in John 3:2, *We know that thou art a teacher come from God: for no man can do these miracles that thou doest, except God be with him.*"

I stared hard at my coffee.

"Not that I blame you. We're quite a handful, the four of us but—well, here, let me show you."

He rose from his chair and crossed to the door leading from our back room into his shop. When he opened it, the muffled rattling I heard grew louder. I followed him as he flipped on the fluorescent lights to reveal a small store, twenty by thirty foot. It smelled of sage, old wood, and oil. The counters and shelves were stacked with all manner of rings, bolo ties, blankets, turquoise jewelry, and cactus terrariums. There were dozens of geodes—some small, some large. There outsides were nondescript gray and brown. But inside, when split open they revealed a profusion of sparkling quartz. I was stopped by one the size of a basketball—the whites, blues, and pink crystals exploding like a starburst.

"She's a beaut, ain't she? But sometimes," he pointed to the brown, outer layer, "sometimes you gotta get past the outside to see the real glory inside." I nodded. "But come over here, I want to show you somethin'."

I followed him past wooden bins of polished stones separated by size and color until we arrived at a work bench and the source of all the noise. It was a small, spinning cylinder attached to a simple motor with a belt. Shouting over it, he asked, "Know what this is?"

"A rock polisher?"

"Tumbler. Yup. Know how it works?"

"Um . . ."

"Like a church." He reached to a larger bin under the counter and scooped up a handful of ordinary rocks. "This is us, all dull, craggy, in some cases just flat-out ugly. And God, he throws us in this tumbler with a little bit of polish and some grit just to irritate us. Then he lets us bang the badness out of each other until . . ." He reached over and snapped off the machine. It came to a blessed, silent stop. He opened the cylinder and pulled out another handful of stones—beautifully polished, some clear, others red, green, or calico.

"Us?" I ventured.

"*Iron sharpeneth iron; so a man sharpeneth the countenance of his friend.* Proverbs 27:17."

I nodded.

"But some," he pushed the stones around in his hand to find a sharp, jagged one, green and broken. "They're no good. Got hidden cracks, runnin' through and through. So be careful."

I looked at him, waiting for more.

"Like candy, they look good on the outside, but inside—" he lifted the fragment between his fingers and tossed it into a waste bin. "Inside she's full of poison. Good for nothin' but the trash heap."

I frowned, not quite making the connection. "Are you talking about someone here?"

"Just be careful."

My frown deepened.

He said nothing but returned to the tumbler.

CHAPTER

THIRTEEN

WE WERE INTERRUPTED by the jingling of a small bell above the front door. I turned to see Darlene enter the shop.

"There you are?" she said. Holding up two bottles of wine, she added, "Victoria sent me on a liquor run to Sophia's Bar."

"Victoria . . ." Cowboy shook his head, quoting, *"And be not drunk with wine; wherein is excess."*

I traded looks with Darlene who brushed off the comment. "Right. Beautiful shop you got here."

"Just lookin' for ways to share the Lord's glory."

"Well," she stooped to examine the closest geode, "whatever you're sharing, it's impressive." She rose and turned to me. "Been a few months. Any chance of walking a gal home and catching up a little?"

"We was jus wrappin' up," Cowboy said as he turned to the tumbler and snapped it back on.

Taking my cue, I wished him a good evening and headed outside with Darlene. We strolled toward

Victoria's—a custom home of glass and steel, sitting atop a flat outcropping of rock. On the horizon a three-quarter moon, barely visible, glowed amber-red. Overhead stars were nearly nonexistent.

"Listen," I said. "I really appreciate your coming all the way out here."

"No problem. Just your everyday airline flight with a screaming baby and sulking teen, followed by a car rental breaking down every forty miles, and a marathon, butt-busting ride that will keep my chiropractor busy for years."

"That bad, huh?"

"If you can't make a girl's life miserable, what good are you?"

"Thank you."

"You're welcome."

After a moment I said, "Billie-Jean is looking good. When did she start walking?"

"Around her first birthday."

I sighed. "Which I also missed." Darlene remained quiet, letting the silence speak for itself. "Everything else good?" I asked. "Back home, I mean?"

"The Olsen kid is looking after your dog, Siggy. Patricia plans to swing by from time to time to check up on the place."

"Patricia," I repeated. "How is she?"

"Still got a rod up her rear, if that's what you mean?" I nodded. Darlene had never been shy about her opinions of Patricia. "And with all the stunts you're pulling I wouldn't be sending out wedding invitations just yet."

"Patricia and I are not romantically—"

"Right. Keep saying that and someday you'll believe it."

"She's pretty upset with me?"

"No more than the rest of the country."

"The drought," I said.

"You've made the 1930s' Dust Bowl look like child's play. Farmers can't plant crops. Food prices are going through the roof. Every area in North America has been registering near zero humidity. Zero."

"Wait a minute," I argued, "I got hit by a giant haboob."

"Your point?"

"They only come with thunderstorms." I motioned to the darkened sky. "And what about all this haze?"

"Haze? That's not haze. It's dust."

"What?"

I looked up as she continued. "It's the same across the country. Snowpacks are melting, nothing to replenish them. West Coast is in a perpetual fire season. Weather patterns are off the grid."

"Global warming."

"Global warming is not standing up in a bus shouting, 'In the name of Jesus I command the rain to stop!'"

"You saw that?"

"Everybody saw it. Crazies are screaming, 'It's God's judgment! The end of the world!' People are flocking to churches, synagogues, mosques. Your evangelical buddies are cleaning up."

"It wasn't my . . . it can't be my doing."

"Good luck with that. The healings, raising people from the dead, the stunt with that kid in Vegas. Like it or not, you're the designated Miracle Man."

I stared hard at the ground, trying to piece it all together. After several moments she spoke again. A bit kinder. "Something's different about you, though, I'll give you that. And I'm not talking about this scrawny, new body of yours and that no-nothing butt."

I adjusted my baggy shirt and hiked up my sagging pants—even end-time prophets have some dignity. "Desert living," I said. "Not the best weight-loss program."

"It's more than that."

"Meaning . . . ?" I turned to her and waited.

Darlene shook her head. "I don't know. It's like you're more at peace now, more comfortable in your own skin. As if you finally figured out who Will Thomas is."

I frowned, remembering the number of times Yeshua said we'd be working on that exact thing, my identity.

She looked at me, waiting for a reply. I shrugged. "I've had a lot of God time."

"Still blaming him, are you?"

I wasn't sure how to respond. She saved me the effort. "After all you've been through, how on earth you can keep getting back on that horse, and with all this, this . . . faith. It's beyond me. Who knows, you might make a believer out of me yet."

"Careful," I said, "it's a slippery slope."

"Not to worry. Whenever I think of drinking the Kool-Aid," she motioned to the rock shop, "people like Gustoff Rutherford, there, remind me of reality."

"He's a little old-school, I'll give you that. But he knows his Bible."

"And I know his type."

"Come again?"

"He's all about God and religion on the outside, but inside . . ." she simply shook her head. "But you . . . for you, it's like an inside job. Granted, on the outside, you're still a piece of work, sometimes a major piece of work. But inside . . ." She took a breath and said nothing, letting the phrase hang.

I wasn't sure how to respond and was smart enough not to try. But as we walked in silence, I knew she was right. Something had happened—and was continuing to happen. Yeshua talked about fast-growing weeds versus slow-growing trees. Well, if he wanted slow-learning trees growing at glacial speeds, I was his man.

But me running a church? Seriously, wasn't creating the universe in six days enough of a challenge?

CHAPTER
FOURTEEN

AFTER LOOKING IN on sleeping Billie-Jean who had only grown prettier the last several months—and, no, I couldn't wake her and, yes, we could play tomorrow if I promised to shave and stop looking like a homeless man—I left the luxury of what Victoria called her "little hideaway" and stepped outside. The night had not cooled. I stuffed my hands into my pockets and started back down the road to my own luxurious quarters when I heard the crunch of sand and gravel beside me. I turned to see Yeshua in standard-issue sandals and robe.

"You're back." I tried sounding casual; no easy task when walking beside the Savior of the world.

"I never leave you."

And I never win that argument, so why try.

"How are you doing?" he asked.

"Oh, you know."

"Yes, I do."

I sighed, then looked up at the sky. "Is this . . . what Darlene said and the others, am I really responsible for this?"

"I promised you big things."

"Right, but this?"

"I've done all I can to warn the world I love so deeply. Now it's time to get her attention."

"The drought?"

"For starters."

"Starters? That doesn't sound good."

"It won't be."

"Because of all the evil around us? The immorality?"

"Immorality is only a symptom."

"Of?"

"Hearts filled with adultery."

"Adultery?" I chewed on the phrase, suspecting he was talking more than just sex. "Like loving the world instead of you?" I asked.

"Which, like all sexual promiscuity, eventually contracts the world's disease."

That shut me up. We walked in a long moment of silence before I spoke again. "And me leading some sort of church is supposed to change all that?"

"You need to experience my passion before declaring my wrath."

"Wrath?"

"Will . . ." he turned to me and I was startled by his eyes. Instead of the usual twinkle they were swollen with the same emotion I'd seen in Las Vegas. "For you to understand my fury, you must understand the depth of my love. Your heart must be broken by what breaks my heart."

I frowned, not understanding, or at least hoping I hadn't. "No way am I qualified to run a church," I said. "Or cause a drought. Or do whatever else this thing is you have planned."

"No, you're not."

"Then—"

"I am."

I shook my head. "You don't understand—" and was blinded by sunlight. It was midday and we stood in another desert. On a rocky slope similar to what I'd seen from Elijah's cave. Only Elijah wasn't there. Instead, it was an older man, barefoot, stooped, and supporting himself on a staff. More importantly, he was talking to a bush, a stunted tree. And it was on fire.

I whispered in awe, "Is that . . . Moses?"

"Yes," he whispered back. "Listen, carefully."

The old man's voice trembled as he spoke, "Who am I? Who am I that I should go to Pharaoh?"

"Sound familiar?" Yeshua asked. I was too struck by the moment to respond. He tried again. "Will?"

I blinked, coming to. "Sorry?"

"Does his reluctance sound familiar?"

I scowled, then shook my head. "No way. You can't compare me to Moses."

"As I said, it's not about you. Or Moses." He spoke again, only this time his voice was not only beside me but also inside the flames: "I will be with you."

Overwhelmed, I closed my eyes.

A moment passed and Moses spoke again. "Suppose I go to the Israelites and say to them, 'The God of your fathers has sent me to you,' and they ask me, 'What is his name?' Then what shall I tell them?"

Once again Yeshua spoke—beside me and within the flames. "I am who I am. This is what you are to say to the Israelites: 'I am has sent me to you.'"

I found it difficult to breathe.

"Hang in there, Will."

When I could finally speak, I said, "'I am who I am.' What does that even mean?"

"In Hebrew my name is spelled, 'Y-H-W-H.'"

I noticed it had no vowels and said, "How can you pronounce something with no vowels? It sounds more like breathing than speaking."

"Exactly," he said. "Try it."

"Try what?"

"Breathing in."

I hesitated. He gave me a nod of encouragement. I opened my mouth and took a small, tentative breath.

"Now," he said, "breathe out." He nodded again and I exhaled.

"Do you hear it?" he asked. "Yhhh . . . Whhh. Try again, only listen."

I breathed in again, and this time heard the, "Yhhh . . ." And, breathing out, I heard, "Whhh."

"Again. Deeper."

I nodded, breathing in, "Yhhh," and out, "Whhh."

"Faster."

"YH WH . . . YHWH." I turned to Yeshua, astonished.

"That's who I am, Will. Life. Its very essence. Every living being that breathes says my name a thousand times a day. Whoever they are, whatever they're doing, I AM."

If I was stunned before, I was speechless now. Was it possible? He was everywhere. Not just the Savior of the world but encompassing everything around me. And in me.

But the lesson still wasn't over. I focused back on Moses just in time to hear him say, "What if they do not believe me or listen to me and say, 'The Lord did not appear to you'?"

I turned back to Yeshua. "That's exactly my point," I said. "What proof do I have that—"

"Shh," he motioned for silence. Then he spoke again—to me and through the flames. "What is that in your hand?"

Moses looked at the rod he was holding. "A staff," he said.

"Throw it on the ground."

Without hesitation, Moses threw it onto the rocks. It barely hit the ground before it morphed into a living snake. He quickly jumped back—well, as quick as an old guy can jump. I also moved away, the bite on my ankle a clear motivator.

"Now," Yeshua said to him. "Reach out your hand and take it by the tail."

At first Moses hesitated the type of thing you'd do, burning bush or not. But Yeshua waited, remaining silent, making it clear he had nothing more to say. Finally, Moses eased up behind the snake. He stooped down, and when he was sure it wasn't looking, he grabbed its tail. And the moment he touched it, it stiffened, straightening back into a staff.

I turned to Yeshua. "And that's going to convince everyone?"

"It's all he has."

"All he has? Then what—" I came to a stop, remembering the lesson from priming the pump, and from the bread and fish. I looked to him and he nodded.

"But . . . what do I have?"

"You have your heart, Will. When you gave it to me, it was as dangerous and deadly as that snake. But you threw it down. You let it die so I could transform it. And that, my dear friend, is what I'll use to change the world."

Suddenly it was night again. We'd returned to the dusty road leading to Sophia's store. Once I got my bearings, which involved trying not to hyperventilate, I said, "You could choose others." I motioned to the rock shop up ahead. "Like Cowboy. He knows his Bible backward and forward. And, unlike me, he's not a coward, he's not afraid to speak up."

"You're right," he said, "Gustoff Rutherford knows the Scriptures."

I waited. "But . . ."

"He has not given me his heart."

"He's not—how do you know?"

"He uses his Bible and my words to shield himself."

"From?"

"Me."

"I don't understand."

"Like that snake, man's flesh is a writhing, clever creature. It will do anything it can to stay alive—even become religious."

I took another breath, realizing I'd have even more to unpack. But Yeshua wasn't finished. "Sadly, unless the flesh is dead, unless it's fallen to the ground and into my hands, it can never be fully contained. It will always find a crack inside a person's soul to push through and attempt to control it."

I heard soft creaking and looked over to see the door of Fern's camper open. I watched as Cowboy emerged. He didn't see me as he slicked back his hair, put on his hat, and shuffled up the road to his cabin.

I spun back to Yeshua who was gone. But of course, he wasn't.

FIFTEEN

WHOEVER THINKS BEING a church leader (I still don't deserve the word "pastor") is simply giving Sunday talks and smiling when you'd rather punch out someone, is just as clueless as I was. When I agreed to the job (if not saying "no" is agreeing), I figured it was only a matter of dusting off some talks I gave at the Snohomish Correctional Institute back home. Hey, I'm a college professor, I know how to deliver lectures. Little did I realize it had as much to do with touching hearts as reaching minds. And by Yeshua calling his followers "sheep," I realized he was not necessarily praising their intelligence or their ability to play nice. Patricia's pastor once called church a hospital, not a museum. And I soon became its nurse, physician, administrator, therapist, janitor, and head of HR.

It started out with just the eight of us, which proved plenty. Time had not changed Chip or Amber. Chip still had an answer for everything and Amber an argument. Darlene was in charge of our nursery, which meant watching Billie-Jean up at Victoria's house, staying as far from our meetings as possible.

I could always count on Cowboy fact-checking my use of Scripture—keeping in mind God only spoke King James. And, yes, like it or not, I felt obliged to have a few words about his late-night visit to Fern. Well, I had a few words. He had several more, particularly about questioning his integrity and how he had merely dropped off a package misdelivered by Amazon. Yes, Amazon—proof Briarwood was vaguely connected to civilization. We also had a long dialogue (actually, monologue from Cowboy) on how Fern had no business attending church until she repented of her sins.

For her part, Fern was silent and aloof and the few times I could get her to smile felt like a victory. I wasn't keen on how quickly she and Amber paired up until I realized it was really about Billie-Jean. It seemed Fern couldn't get enough of the child. It only made sense when Sophia confided that a past STD (a hazard of Fern's trade) destroyed the possibility of her ever having children of her own.

And, speaking of Sophia—as the self-appointed spokesperson for Mother Earth, she picked and chose Scriptures like a biblical buffet, selecting those that suited her and ignoring those that didn't—often seasoned with a dash of her favorite Eastern philosophies. As a card-carrying, non-confrontationist I was able to side-step many of her New Age arguments—except when it came to reincarnation. I recounted how Joseph Namaliu, Patricia's friend, shared his story of the orphaned children in rural Nepal eating dirt to fill their bellies. And how the villagers felt they exhibited more love by refusing to help the children, allowing them to suffer and die more quickly. The reason? The children must have done something terrible in a past life to be orphaned in this one. And the sooner they paid for their karma by suffering and dying, the sooner they could reincarnate to a better future.

Sophia's response was a sigh which turned into one of her hacking coughs. Coming up for air, she managed to say, "And now you're going to tell me Jesus died to pay for their sins, right?"

I nodded and explained, "The two beliefs cannot coexist. Either Jesus lied when he said he died for all of our sins or he told the truth."

If I scored any points with Sophia, she was too seasoned to let on. But at least I was getting bolder with the truth. And not for argument's sake. Instead, to my surprise, it was coming from love. A love that, despite the group's idiosyncrasies (and there were many), kept deepening. I remember some Trappist monk writing, "Go into the desert not to escape other men but in order to find them in God." Maybe that's what was happening to me.

"If you love me, feed my sheep." Isn't that what Yeshua said to Peter? Yes, the group was self-centered and prickly and quarrelsome and—did I mention self-centered? But the more time I spent with them, the deeper my love grew. And the deeper I fell in love with them, the deeper I fell in love with God. Or maybe it was the other way around. Or maybe it was the same.

Oddly enough, Victoria, who would be the most instrumental in it all tumbling down, was also the neediest. And it wasn't her drink or her hedonism. It was living in a world where money was king. And since bigger was always better, why would it be any different with the church? She soon began purchasing social media ads and even radio spots about the famous prophet now preaching in Briarwood. She also hired the best musicians from nearby towns to ensure we had the appropriate entertainment.

On more than one late-night talk at Sophia's Bar and Grill—Victoria with her drinks and Darlene hanging around to "chaperone"—I explained that her tactics were not exactly how Jesus intended to grow the kingdom of God. I spoke how it should be his Spirit who is the attraction, his ability to change people from the inside out. I mentioned Yeshua's analogy of balloons, and Sophia managed to dig up a couple for me to demonstrate.

"We're like this balloon," I said holding up a deflated one. "We have all the makings for life, but when we try to live it . . ." I tossed the balloon into the air and it fell to the ground. "We have nothing inside. Sure, we can fill ourselves with money and booze and material things, anesthetizing ourselves so we don't feel the emptiness, but those things never last. They always rot or rust."

Darlene chuckled. "And let's not forget the morning afters."

Victoria raised her glass in a toast. "Praise God for Tylenol."

I scooped up the balloon and continued. "But if we allow God to fill us . . ." I put it to my mouth and blew until it was full. "His Spirit not only pushes against the outside pressures trying to crush us . . ." I tied it off and began bouncing it into the air. "He replaces that inside emptiness with his life. Instead of our feeble attempts, he fills us with his peace and his joy and his goodness."

I thought it a pretty good speech. I would have been more encouraged if Victoria hadn't immediately ordered several cartons of party balloons to offer as free give-aways. Still, it was better than her earlier plan of Denny's dinner coupons to the first thirty who showed.

And show they did. Within two weeks we outgrew the back of Cowboy's rock shop and graduated to Sophia's bar, complete with tin ceiling, overhead lamps on wagon wheels, and the usual mounted heads. Cowboy voiced disapproval of the mirrored wall of lighted liquor bottles as well as the red neon Budweiser sign. But he could live with the karaoke stage where, after they were carefully vetted, I delivered my sermons.

Despite the growing crowd, they came mostly out of curiosity. For those up front, cell phones were discreetly slipped from pockets, while those in back felt less inclined to hide them. But it was neither Victoria's advertising nor my carefully crafted sermons that drew them. It was the novelty of seeing the miracle-working prophet who raised people from the dead and called down the wrath of God.

Any hope of shaking hands at the end of the service and wishing people a good day was replaced by Q and A's:

"Are you aware how bad you're making God look?"

"Who made you judge?"

"This is America. You can't expect me to suffer for other people's sins."

And my favorite: "They stoned false prophets in the Bible."

Two of my most devoted attendees arrived the first week in suits and ties. After that it was newly purchased boots, jeans, and bolo ties. They never stopped to shake hands or mingle. And they were always the first to dawn sunglasses and depart in some late-model vehicle unfit for desert terrain.

As the weeks progressed, I never felt unsafe, though I do remember one service being particularly spirited.

Delbert Haas, a prospector and not-so-recovered alcoholic, was more eager than normal to sit up front and share a running commentary on my sermon. Sadly, he was not as eager to be escorted outside by Cowboy and Chip. There was a minor skirmish which ended with Sophia having to apply her first-aid training along with a couple bar towels.

After the meetings I often headed to Victoria's to spend a little R 'n' R with Billie-Jean. I'd missed so much of her first year. And now she had entered that incurably cute age of unsteady steps and incoherent ramblings—not unlike my own the first few minutes of every morning.

It was here I ran into Luna Piper, a reporter Victoria either befriended or paid. She was a tiny, spark plug of a girl with a nasal twang and the social skills of a starved Doberman. After introductions we sat in the kitchen over coffee and tea. It was too early for drinks even by Victoria's standards. She'd barely finished pouring the coffee, some special Arabian blend, before Piper's recorder was out and the inquisition began:

"How do you substantiate your claims of actually hearing God? Is this the same God who told you to support your professor friend who was charged with sexual harassment? Did this God tell you to start the prison riot in Washington State? Was it his idea to heal the killer of Trevor Hunter's wife on national TV?"

The interrogation would have continued had not Darlene entered the room. As soon as she realized what was happening, she was in Piper's face. "I don't know who the (insert expletive) you are or what (insert expletive) you're pulling but—"

"My name is—"

"I don't give a (insert expletive) who you are!" (Darlene held a black belt in expletives.)

But Piper was no amateur. Unfazed, she turned her recorder on Darlene and said, "And your name, please? And, if you wouldn't mind spelling it, to ensure I—"

She saw no need to continue, particularly when Darlene slapped the recorder out of her hand and sent it crashing into the doublewide Viking refrigerator.

"Seriously?" Piper scorned.

"Seriously," Darlene seethed.

Victoria scampered over to scoop it up. "Here, I think it's still—"

"Don't bother," Darlene said. There was something in her voice that told Victoria it was a good idea to forget it. There was something in her glare that made Piper glance over her shoulder and measure the distance to the back kitchen door.

I cleared my throat. "Listen, it's been a long day. Maybe we can continue this conversation another time."

Piper looked from me to Darlene and then to Victoria who was stooping down to the recorder. "If it's broken, we can buy another. I mean these things happen, right?"

"It's time you leave," Darlene said.

Piper held her look, unflinching. It was a standoff until Piper's phone rang. Keeping her eye on Darlene, she pulled it from her pocket.

"Perhaps I didn't make myself clear," Darlene said.

"I heard you." Piper paused to read the phone's ID. "But your boyfriend, here, may want to take this." She passed it over to me.

I frowned, taking it into my hands. "Who is it?"

"Your preacher pal, Trevor Hunter."

CHAPTER
SIXTEEN

I PRESSED THE phone to my ear and answered, "Trevor?"

"Sorry you couldn't make it to the funeral."

"Trevor, I . . ." Unsure how to respond, I settled for a cliche, "How are you?"

"No longer considering suicide, if that's what you mean."

I took a breath, buckling in for the assault. "Yeah. Listen, I never got to say how sorry I was."

"A little preoccupied from what I can remember." I deserved that and more. Refusing to heal someone's wife while raising her killer from the dead brings out the worst in people.

"Look," I said, "I know none of it made sense."

"Nothing you do makes sense." Another accurate observation. "And now, you're taking credit for a worldwide drought?"

"I'm not taking credit for—"

"Do you have any idea how much damage it's causing?"

"I—"

"And not just here. It's spreading—South America, across the ocean to Africa, Asia, Russia."

I closed my eyes, quietly whispering, "God's wrath."

"Say again?"

"I think it's God's way of getting our attention."

"Yeah," Trevor answered, his sarcasm returning. "He sure knows how to do that, doesn't he."

"I'm sorry," I repeated.

"Governor Proctor and I would like to speak with you."

"Governor Proctor?"

"We'd like to sit down, come to some sort of agreement with you. An understanding."

"I'm not the one to talk to."

"He's going to be president, you understand that, right? He's way ahead in the polls. He's already been endorsed by the current administration."

Recalling Chip's comments, I added, "And you may become his vice president."

"You wouldn't hear me complain. But he's holding that card close to his vest, at least until the convention."

"Things haven't changed, have they, Trevor?" He grew silent and, to my surprise, I continued with my recently discovered boldness. Or maybe it was compassion. "You're still searching for affirmation, aren't you? The bigger the better."

"It's not about me, Will. It's about turning our country back to God. The governor is Christian too, you know."

I did. I also knew they were a sizeable voting bloc he was courting. Why else would the great TV preacher, Trevor Hunter, be considered as his running mate. I knew something else as well. I knew the darkness I'd seen surrounding Trevor's compound in Malibu, and I knew the hideous creatures morphing across Proctor's face in Las Vegas.

Without missing a beat, Trevor continued, "We'll e-mail the tickets to Sacramento. I'll even include your little pal, Chet."

"Chip," I corrected.

Ignoring me, he continued, "As you can imagine, the governor's schedule is full, but he made an opening for you this Saturday. The three of us will sit down over breakfast and work something out."

"Work what out?"

"This curse, this whatever it is you're doing."

"It's not me. I'm not doing—"

"Right."

"Trevor, there are some things even politics can't—"

"We'll fly you in Friday, put you up someplace nice, and see you first thing in the morning."

I took a breath. I closed my eyes. Then I gave the only answer I could. "No."

"What?"

"I'm sorry, Trevor. God is not somebody to negotiate with." I held my ground, caving only slightly. "Besides, I've got my group that meets on Sundays."

"Change it."

"It's church."

"Get someone to fill in."

I hesitated.

"Okay, fine," he said. "I'll check his schedule and get back to—"

"I'm sorry, Trevor. Unless I hear different, I'm staying put."

"We're talking about Robert Proctor, governor of the state of California. The future president of the United States!"

"I'm sorry," I repeated. Then, as trite as it sounded, I meant it when I added, "You're in my prayers." There was a moment's silence. Before I could change my mind, I said, "Goodbye, Trevor," and ended the call. I sat a moment. I may be getting a little backbone, but it didn't stop my hand from trembling as I handed the phone back to Piper. Nor did it stop the sadness welling up inside. Just as the months in the desert changed me, apparently Trevor's new life in politics changed him.

❧

The following weeks went as expected—or as I found in the life of pastors, unexpected. Visitors and the curious came and went, often with biting questions and accusations, but the core eight remained. Not that they had any place to go. But they remained. And listened. And asked questions. And I continued falling in love. If this is what Yeshua meant about experiencing his heart, he described it perfectly. It did nothing to stop our little church from being a hospital, but it did make visiting and treating the patients rewarding. No. More than rewarding. For me it became life giving.

But also draining. It was a paradox. Pouring myself into them was fulfilling and exhausting. Infuriating and heartbreaking. I found myself having to go on multiple trips into the desert just for a little solitude. Mini retreats. Several times I tried finding my old cabin—to think, to meditate and to retrieve my stacks of written legal pads. But I could never find it. It was either buried by the haboob or the smaller sandstorms that came more and more frequently, or . . . Well, despite my best efforts, it was never found.

Darlene became more and more of an associate. Whether it was befriending Victoria, the abandoned trophy wife, or sharing war stories with Sophia, or taking Fern under her wing, she was always there.

My visions and visits with Yeshua seemed to be coming to an end. Who needed special visits when I constantly saw glimmers of him in our community. There was, however, one exception. A few days after Trevor's phone call I was up at Victoria's visiting Amber and Billie-Jean, along with the always-present and always-sullen Fern. Despite Cowboy's efforts to separate the group from her, Fern had become part of Billie-Jean's, Amber's, and Darlene's family. Not Chip's or mine, since we were men and could not be trusted, but she had definitely entered their inner circle.

I was sitting on Victoria's plush, living room carpet playing with Billie-Jean as she waddled drunkenly from person to person, handing us toys and taking them back again. It was the highlight of my day and by the smile flickering across Fern's face, I suspected hers as well. But in the middle of our play, I suddenly saw Fern surrounded by bubbles. Hundreds of them, shimmering and translucent, each connected to the other, clinging to her and covering her like thick padding. I sensed they were protecting her, insulating her from the outside world. But they were also her prison, preventing her from touching or being touched by others.

Looking closer, I saw people inside the bubbles. Actually, only two. They moved and spoke inside each of them, playing out scenes over and over again. One was always Fern; her actions so lewd and sexual I figured they were scenes with past clients and lovers. Before I could look away, I noticed the Fern in each scene was of a younger age. Sometimes a teen, sometimes a little girl as young as seven or eight. And she wasn't with different men. Just one. And he was scolding her, always scolding: "Bad girl. You disgust me. Daddy hates it when you make me do this."

Sensing my gaze, Fern turned and caught me staring. Instantly, the bubbles expanded, thickening the barrier between us. We both looked away, embarrassed. Moments later, as I received a plush toy from Billie-Jean and returned it, I thought of Yeshua's response, back when I grilled him about evil in the world. "Why would God allow this type of thing to happen?" I demanded.

"Free will," he said. "My greatest gift to mankind. Without it, you'd simply be robots, programmed with no ability to make choices."

"But the victims?" I argued. "Don't they get to make choices?"

"And where do I draw the line, Will? Where should I make it impossible to do evil?"

"Okay, okay," I said. "But you can at least help, right? When victims cry out to you, you should be able to step in there and help."

"I should."

"Why don't you?" I asked.

"Why don't you?"

"Me? I'm not God."

"You're my feet and hands. Your actions are my actions. Your help, my help. Your love, my love."

"Yes," I nodded. "But only if I choose."

"Exactly. My greatest gifts—love and free will."

I frowned. "So . . . you're telling me the question isn't, 'Why, God?' The question is really . . ." I paused, thinking it through.

"Yes." His answer was gentle and sad. "The question isn't, 'Why, God?' it's, 'Why, man?'"

Recalling the memory, I watched Billie-Jean stagger toward Fern. The young woman was still enveloped in the bubbles, still the trapped prisoner inside—until Billie-Jean stretched out her little hand and gave her the toy. And where Billie-Jean touched, where the two made contact, the bubbles popped and thinned. Of course, others rushed in, moving and expanding to take their place. But in that one small area, in that one moment of love, they had disappeared.

SEVENTEEN

TO THEIR CREDIT, the sheriff's department waited outside Sophia's Bar 'n' Church until I finished the service. But when they did enter, they compensated with more than enough melodrama.

"Dr. William Thomas, you are under arrest!"

There were startled gasps as the congregation turned. A few rose—mostly to step aside to leave a clear and unencumbered path to me. (I may have mentioned, they were not the most dedicated flock.) There were four officers. They could have done it with one. Not that I didn't have defenders: Chip, Cowboy, and Sophia. Amber and Darlene were with Billie-Jean up at Victoria's where the woman was sleeping off another Saturday night. And Fern? After seeing the uniformed officers, she immediately vanished, memories clearly too fresh.

They were six feet from my karaoke stage when Cowboy stepped between us, his formidable size bringing them to a stop. "Just what are you fellas up to?"

The oldest officer, a graying man with drooping eyes, spoke, "Step aside, sir."

Cowboy held his gaze and did not move.

Attempting to avoid trouble, the officer spoke past Cowboy directly to me. "William Thomas, you are under arrest for multiple violations of building and safety codes."

Cell phones were out all around.

"What type of violations?" Cowboy said.

"I'm speaking to Dr. Thomas."

"What type," Cowboy repeated.

"This building is not zoned for a church."

I started to answer, but Cowboy cut me off. "Not zoned for a church? But it's okay for a bar?"

"Don't worry," I said, stepping from the stage. "It's just a misunderstanding. I'm sure we can clear it—"

"Safety codes?" Cowboy repeated.

"And parking regulations," the officer replied.

"Parking! We live in the desert."

I raised my hands. "Gentlemen, please, we can—"

"I don't make the rules, sir. Now step aside."

"This ain't nothin' but the state tryin' to take away our religious freedom." Cowboy turned to the crowd. "Are we gonna let 'em do that, people?"

The people gave no response—save a few nervous coughs and the repositioning of phones for a better angle.

"Well, are we?"

The officer's voice hardened. "I do not make the laws, sir. I merely enforce them."

"Yeah, well this time you won't be."

"Is that a threat?"

"It's standin' up for our God-given rights."

The officer had enough. He turned to two of his younger colleagues and with a nod to Cowboy ordered, "Arrest him."

"Listen," I said, "I'm more than willing—" But the order had been given and the two moved in.

"Get your hands off me," Cowboy shouted as they attempted to grab him. "I said—" he threw an elbow into the chest of one and turned for the other.

"Stop!" I shouted.

He reared back his free arm but they caught it. He tried twisting away as the fourth officer rushed in.

"Stop this!" I shouted, stepping into the fray. "Stop—"

The commander grabbed me as if I had joined in the fight. I turned, instinctively protecting myself, and the brawl was in full swing—as brief as it was. Within moments both Cowboy and I found our arms behind our backs, hands bound together with plastic zip ties. We were quickly escorted past the crowd and cellphones toward the door, Sophia dogging them the whole way. "This is my establishment! These are my guests!"

I remember Chip shouting, "His rights, you haven't read him his Mirandas!" And later, as they eased me into the back seat of one of the cars, he was shouting, "Don't talk to anyone, Uncle Will! Not without a lawyer! You got your rights. Trust me, I know how this works!"

◈

Arroyo Sisco was a thirty-five-minute drive and the closest town with the facilities necessary to hold dangerous criminals such as Cowboy and myself. Compared to Briarwood, Arroyo Sisco was a bustling metropolis. Paved roads (both of them), a blinking signal/stoplight, and a jail with two separate cells—one for Cowboy who, thankfully talked himself into momentary exhaustion, and one for me to share with the town drunk, Harry Malachi Buchanan.

Harry was a prospector who had great success finding silver and, later, uranium over forty years ago. But as a self-proclaimed desert rat, he knew his luck would change any day.

"Just a matter of waiting it out," he said.

I nodded, knowing all about waiting.

"What you in for?" His cough was worse than Sophia's but with the added attraction of bringing up a wad of phlegm. And swallowing.

When I told him, he immediately saw the picture. "You're that prophet dude, the one who caused this drought." I sighed. Seriously, was there anyone who hadn't heard? Harry shook his head, chuckling, which turned into another rasping cough. "And you think they got you in jail cause of breaking some ordinance? Roy and the boys, they're all eager to make arrests and everything but not that eager. Something else is goin' on."

I frowned. "Like what?"

"You got the whole nation pissed at you and you think you're in here for breaking safety codes?" He coughed and swallowed. "Either you're the humblest man I ever seen or the stupidest."

I knew where I'd cast my vote.

"At least you ain't no glory hound, I'll give you that. Holdin' up out there in the middle of nowhere actin' all pious."

I nodded, unsure how to handle the compliment—if it was a compliment. He motioned me across the cell to the lower bunk. I obeyed, taking the two or three necessary steps.

"Sit, sit," he said.

I sat.

"But if you want humble, I mean real humbleness, I got one for you. Story, I mean. From my indigenous friends."

"Okay . . ."

"If you got the time."

I shrugged, figuring I could squeeze him into my busy schedule.

"Well then." He coughed. But this time he crossed to the rusty sink and spat. Wiping his chin, he turned back to me and began:

"Seems when the Great Spirit was busy creatin', he put Wind, Fire, and Water out there on their own to see who was the most powerful."

I listened politely.

"So Wind, he comes back braggin' 'bout all the destruction he done with his storms and tornadoes and such. How he'd parched up the land with the heat of his breath and killed with blasts of freezing cold.

"And the Great Spirit, he's pretty impressed and he turns to Fire. And Fire, she tells how she set whole forests ablaze, how she destroyed homes and fields and cities. How she terrified men wherever she went.

"And the Great Spirit, he's even more impressed. Then he turns to Water. 'And what about you?' he says.

"And Water, he looks down all embarrassed. 'I can't do nothin' like that,' he says. 'I got no power.'

"And the Spirit, he smiles kindly. 'Oh, but you're mistaken,' he says. 'You got the greatest power of all. By takin' the lowest position, you seeped unseen into the cracks of rocks, splittin' 'em apart when you freeze. And your streams, they change the earth, sometime slow but always constant. And, unnoticed, you sink deep down into the roots of living things, givin' life to all you touch. By takin' the lowest position of all, you have the greatest power.'"

I sat staring at Harry, wondering if the old-timer had any idea of the depth he'd just spoken. He gave me the slightest nod, coughed, and turned back to the sink.

EIGHTEEN

IT WASN'T MUCH of a plan, but Chip might have pulled it off save one minor hitch.

It was late afternoon. Deputy Roy, a good-natured man, muscular but with plenty of cream filling in the middle, assured us that first thing Monday morning, the judicial system would rise from its Sunday slumber and we could post bail.

"Why everybody's so gung-ho about getting you arrested today is beyond me." He propped his boots up on the desk and reached for the TV remote. "But when duty calls."

"Who exactly made that call?" Cowboy asked from his cell.

Roy shrugged. "Someone yanking the sheriff's chain. Listen, you fellas want me to order you something? Theresa, down at Sparrow's Nest, she's a pretty good cook."

"Chicken fried steak's good," Harry said.

Eating was not exactly on my bucket list. But it didn't matter because Chip suddenly burst through the front door. "Someone's broken into CVS!" he cried.

Roy sat up. "What?"

"Down the street. They threw a rock through the window. Bet they're going after the drugs."

Roy was on his feet. "We'll see about that!" Scooping his hat off the desk, he headed for the door.

"Better hurry," Chip called. "Don't know how long they been there." Once Roy exited, Chip turned to us with a grin. "Not bad, huh?"

"What are you doing?" Cowboy demanded.

Chip crossed to Roy's desk and began rummaging through the drawers. "Breaking you out."

"Breaking us out?" I exclaimed.

"Sophia's in the car out back." Finished with the drawers, he moved to the filing cabinet behind him.

"Chip—"

"Any idea where he keeps the keys?"

"Where he keeps the . . ." I let the comment fade.

He rifled through the papers on top. When he saw nothing he turned, scanning the room. "A hook, a peg on the wall, or something?"

"Son," Cowboy said, "this ain't no Western."

"Keypad!" Harry motioned to the wall beside us. "On that wall over there."

"A keypad," Chip repeated as he moved to the adjacent wall just out of sight. "Right."

I pressed my face against the bars, trying to see.

"Now I just need the code."

And there was the hitch. I heard beeping as he tried one combo after another.

"Chip," I said. "We'll be out in the morning. Let it be."

But the beeping continued. "Anybody know the cop's birthday?"

"You don't have time," Cowboy argued. "There's a thousand possibilities."

"September," Harry said.

"Great." Chip continued pressing keys.

"Or October."

The beeping continued. "It's four digits. I just need the right combo."

"0610."

Startled, we all turned to see Roy reenter the room.

"That's my anniversary. 0610. Try it." Chip hesitated. "Go ahead."

Chip entered the number, and I heard the buzz-click of my cell door unlocking.

"Now go over there and pull it open."

Reluctantly obeying, Chip asked, "Did you, uh, catch those guys?"

"Step inside."

"Look," Chip stalled, "I really hope you caught them 'cause—"

"Inside."

Chip entered my cell.

"Close it, please."

He reached out and pulled the door shut.

"Thank you." After a moment, Roy added, "So, how 'bout that chicken fried steak? Any takers?"

❧

Taking pity on Chip (or was it me?), Roy moved him to Cowboy's cell so we could each have a bunk. I didn't sleep well, but not for reasons you'd expect. A year ago, I'd have been pacing the floor all night, eaten up with worry. But now . . . Of course, I was confused and perplexed (welcome to my world), but I wasn't wrecked with anxiety. Strange. I thought of the balloon analogy, how the outside circumstances were having less and less impact upon my insides.

No, any lack of sleep did not come from worry. It had to do with the chainsaw sleeping in the bunk above me. Then, of course there was the chicken fried steak. There should be a law about feeding the elderly after eight p.m.

Roy woke us up just before sunrise. "Got some good news and some bad news, fellas. The good news is, like I said, it's all gonna be taken care of today. The bad news is they gotta transfer you over to Five Corners where they got the appropriate facilities for processing your bail."

"Five Corners?" Cowboy complained. "That's another hour from here."

"And the faster you get your hind ends to the vehicle waitin' out back, the sooner you'll get there."

"What about me?" Harry asked. "I'm goin' too?"

"No need. You got a runnin' account with the court. They'll put it on your tab."

The predawn air was hot and dusty as Roy led us to the waiting car. Imagine my surprise when I saw it was occupied by the same two men who regularly attended my church and never stuck around to socialize. Today they wore sunglasses with dark suits and ties. Truth be told, they looked more like Men in Black than officers of the law. Actually, considering the cheap cut of their suits, they could have been the Blues Brothers.

"Just him," the driver said, motioning to me.

"What about Rutherford here," Roy asked, "and the kid?"

"Just him."

"But Rutherford resisted arrest. The boy was orchestratin' a jail break." The driver simply looked at Roy. It seemed to be enough. "Well, all right then. Let's go, preacher." Taking my arm, Roy opened the back door and helped me inside.

"No way," Chip stepped toward us. "Where he goes, I go."

Roy turned to him. "You heard the man. You're free."

"I'm staying right here with him." Chip tried moving past Roy. "We're a team."

"Chip," I called from the back.

The front door opened and the driver's partner stepped out, all six feet and some inches of him.

Chip continued, "The dude's old. He needs someone to look after him."

I appreciated the dedication. Not so much the logic.

Roy continued to block him. "And I'm saying you're free to go."

Chip tried again to move past him. "Where he goes, I go."

The partner arrived, but Chip refused to be intimidated, even by him. "There's no way I'm—"

With lightning speed, the big man grabbed Chip and threw him to the ground.

"Come on now," Roy protested, "there ain't no need for that."

The partner ignored him, turned, and headed back to his side of the car.

Cowboy helped Chip to his feet, the boy brushing himself off and shouting, "Police brutality!" Then, spotting a tear in his knee, he cried out, "Look at these pants! They cost me ninety-eight bucks! Police brutality!"

"Chip," Cowboy cautioned.

"I know my rights! Police brutality!"

"Chip!"

Chip turned to him. "What!?"

"Them fellas, they ain't police."

CHAPTER

NINETEEN

WE'D BEEN ON the road a good fifty minutes when the big guy up front passed his cell phone back to me. "For you," he said.

I took it and answered. "Hello?"

"Hey, Miracle Man." It was Trevor Hunter. "How's it going?"

"I've had better days." Watching the men up front, I added, "But I bet you know that."

"Know what?"

I saw no reason to humor him. "So, what are you doing? Kidnapping me?"

"Kidnapping you? No, no, my man. I'm calling to see how I can help you. Rumor has it they're throwing some crazy charges at you."

"Which I'm sure you had nothing to do with."

"Not yet."

"Meaning?"

"Look, Will. I'm not the one who broke the law here. And I certainly didn't invent the charges. But I can make them go away."

"I told you I'm not interested."

"You're forgetting the demonstrations."

"Demonstrations?"

"You're hurting too many people with this drought thing. Costs across the board are skyrocketing. People are pushing back. Angry people."

"I told you it's not my doing."

"Like your refusal to heal my wife?" Before I could answer, he continued. "The point is folks expect the government to do something."

"My talking to the governor won't accomplish anything."

"It's optics, dude. The two of you in the same room, trying to work things out."

"God doesn't negotiate. I told you that. Especially with men like Proctor."

"Because?"

I took a deep breath. "He's . . . evil, Trevor. He may look good on the outside—"

"Which we're counting on for the female vote."

"—but inside, what I saw, inside there's something unhealthy about him. Something dark." There was a long pause. "Trevor?"

Finally he said, "Just talk to him. Come on in and talk, what will it hurt?"

"You have my answer, Trevor."

"And you're sure about that."

"I'm sure."

"Well . . . that's too bad."

"What does that mean?"

"One way or another, when you do change your mind, let me know."

"What does that mean?"

"Goodbye, Will."

"Wait a minute. Hello? Hello?" He was no longer there.

I closed my eyes. From what I'd seen, Governor Proctor was evil; at least he was manipulated by it. I saw the thing morphing over his face in Vegas. I saw its reaction to my presence. And I saw the black cloud of creatures surrounding him. And yet, hadn't I of all people learned that every person has the right to change, to ask for forgiveness and turn around? Was I being too quick to judge? I rubbed my forehead wondering and muttering, "God . . . dear God . . ."

"Present."

I gave a start and opened my eyes to see Yeshua beside me. Regaining my composure, I turned to him and asked, "Is it my imagination or are you showing up less frequently? And, yes, I know you're always with me but I'm talking about these, these—"

"Guest appearances?"

I nodded.

"And don't forget your helper." He motioned to the hood of the car where the Holy Spirit, now as the gymnast I'd first seen in my hospital room, sat cross-legged, enjoying the wind blowing through his hair. "He's always with you too."

I sighed.

"But to answer your question. There's no growth if I keep popping in and micromanaging your every decision."

"It would make things easier."

"Since when is growth easy?"

"I could stand for a little less growth and a little more peace."

"But you have it. Whenever you stop looking at the outside circumstances and trust me."

I nodded. "The balloon analogy."

"My kingdom inside you—"

"—spilling out and doing your will."

"On earth as it is in heaven."

I'd seen this happen enough to know there was no argument. And yet, I shook my head.

"What?"

"How does that help me decide what to do?"

"As I've said, our hearts becoming one will make your choice my choice."

"And your choice is?"

He grinned. "Nice try."

I looked out the window, mumbling, "Can't fault a mortal for trying."

"I'm not a cosmic Ouija Board, Will. I don't give yes and no answers."

"I know, I know," I said, referring to past conversations. "You're not binary. Instead of *A* or *B* your answer can be oranges."

"See, you do have my mind."

I gave another sigh.

"And sometimes my answer is simply wait."

"But for how long? You keep saying that. You even say I'm somehow in the Bible. But for the life of me I can't figure it out."

"If you could, it would be wrong."

"How long?"

"You'll know."

"You'll tell me?"

"You'll know."

I blew out another breath of frustration and looked back out the window. We'd just entered another town; large enough for traffic and more than one stop light.

I felt his hand on my shoulder. "Soon, my friend. Everything is going exactly as planned."

I turned to him. "You saw all this?"

"Before you were born."

"Because you live outside of time."

"Outside of it? I invented it."

The car lurched to a stop. The type of thing you do to avoid hitting people. There were a half dozen of them, purposefully standing in front of us.

I called to the driver, "What's going on?"

Neither man answered.

I turned to Yeshua but he was gone. Then to the hood of the car. So was the Spirit. We began inching forward. No one in the crowd was interested in suicide and when it became clear we weren't stopping, they grudgingly gave ground until we pulled into a parking spot. Above us, loomed a two-story, old brick building.

"Who are these people?" I asked.

The man in the passenger seat, who was already on his phone, paused long enough to answer, "Some of your fans."

"My what?"

He spoke back into the phone, "Understood," then disconnected.

I heard the door beside me unlock as the big man opened his own door and, without expression, pushed his way through the crowd to my side of the car. By now I'd seen enough recorders and cell phones to know they were reporters. When he arrived, he opened my door to the feeding frenzy:

"Dr. Thomas, are you responsible for the drought? How do you justify the suffering of millions? What proof do you have this is God's will? When will you speak with Governor Proctor? What history does your family have of mental illness?"

On and on they went, a blur of words, as my escort helped me out and guided me through the crowd to the building's entrance. I had no idea how they found me until I heard an irritating, nasal twang. "Are you aware this is totally illegal?"

I turned to see Luna Piper, Victoria's reporter friend. With recorder in hand, she shouted at my escort. "Do you know this is a political shakedown?" It was more statement than question. "Half the charges are bogus. Those ordinances aren't even on the books!" Taking the bait, he cut her a look—which is exactly what she wanted. Going in for the kill, she demanded, "Who exactly do you represent? Are you aware this is kidnapping; everyone from the top down is engaged in criminal activity?"

There was a second of silence followed by the crowd lunging forward with a new barrage of questions— no longer aimed at me, but at the big man and all the powers behind him.

CHAPTER
TWENTY

"THANKS FOR PICKING me up," I said to Darlene as we drove back to Briarwood.

"Saving your rear seems to be my life's vocation."

I looked out the window smiling. She was right, of course. But coming to my rescue was not the only reason I caught myself thinking about her more frequently. How strange. It often happened as I worked on my sermons, a part of me wondering what she might think if she ever bothered to show up. Maybe it was because we seemed to be the only two designated adults on the good ship Briarwood. Maybe. But I suspected there was more. I kept seeing an honesty about her I couldn't ignore. Unvarnished, I'll admit. Thanks to her childhood abuse by a deacon uncle, she was no longer a card-carrying Christian. But strip away the crusty surface and underneath there was truth. Her core. And it was rock solid.

"You're right," I agreed. "You've been invaluable. And I can't begin to express how much I appreciate that. How much I appreciate you."

"Will?"

I turned to her.

"Shut up."

Point taken. I changed subjects. "Back there, I don't get it. No fines, no charges. The chief of police couldn't wait to cut me loose and get me out of there."

"That Piper chick, she's a pain, but knows her stuff. And you," she glanced over to me, "talk about backbone. Not sure what you're trying to prove, but you've really become an inspiration." Catching herself and clearing her throat, she quickly added, "To us, I mean. Not just me. I mean to all of us."

"Darlene?

"Yeah?"

"Shut up."

She focused back on the road.

Over the following weeks, Piper showed her stuff, alright. Too well. We were in the national press for days. The internet long after that. Chip found entire sites devoted to us. To me. And, sadly, it took its toll on those of us who simply wanted church. People came hours ahead of time to get a seat. Cowboy and Sophia wired up speakers and Bluetooth so the overflow could listen outside on lawn chairs or in the comfort of air-conditioned cars. Sundays quickly became a circus of the media, the curious, and the angry.

But the drama wasn't limited to those outside our circle. Inside the group, there was plenty of histrionics to go around. And it seemed to grow almost daily. One meeting in particular comes to mind:

"Why can't we charge admission?" Sophia demanded. "I got utility bills." Turning to me, she added, "When you get down to it, I really should be charging you rent."

"Us," Darlene corrected. "We're all in this together."

"I'm sorry," Sophia shot back, "exactly what are you contributing?"

Darlene was about to respond in vintage Darlene, but caught my look and let it go. Not Sophia. "People are in there every week recording and taking pictures. You know they're selling that stuff." She broke into a fit of coughing, then caught her breath long enough to add, "And writing articles, probably books. It's all happening in my place and there's no way I'll see a penny of it."

"We should all have a cut," Chip said. "Sweat equity."

"The Jews do it," Victoria said.

"Do what?" I asked.

"Charge membership. For special synagogue privileges."

"Absolutely not," Cowboy said. "But take an offering, you bet." Turning to me, he added, "You need to start passing the plate; preach on tithing. Malachi 3:8–10."

"And bring in a real band," Victoria said. "None of these sorry locals. I got friends in Vegas who could really draw a crowd."

"I don't think we're looking for a bigger crowd," Darlene said.

Victoria argued, "It's the American way."

To which Chip jumped in, "Maybe Jesus isn't American." That stopped her. Come to think of it, it stopped everyone—except Chip. "God's bigger than just our country, right?"

"Might wanna study your history a bit more carefully, son," Cowboy said. "Ain't no nation on earth more godly and blessed."

Chip countered, "Except when it comes to the homeless. And the immigrants, and health care, and racism, and the military industrial complex, and—" If Chip continued, it was hard to hear over all the indignation.

Until Victoria's voice rose above the din. "Chip's right! Think of the crowd we could draw if we address those issues!"

Darlene fired back, "Are we talking size or issues?"

Amber piped in with all the wisdom of a bumper sticker. "Power corrupts!" Although no one paid her attention, she probably came closest to the truth.

Even silent, sullen Fern had concerns. Her pimp spotted her on the news and was threatening to come and drag her back to LA. "What about security?" she said. "We need to start thinking about security."

Seems everyone had issues. With our explosive growth, what started out as a small community of people—broken people, I'll give you that—became a fractious group of opinions and special interests.

For me, the saddest case was Cowboy and his concern over Fern. More than once he cornered me. "What are we gonna do when people find out we got a practicin' whore in our midst."

"Practicing?" I said.

"Well, that's what they'll say. Don't matter if it's true, you know they'll say it."

And every time I pointed out that people like Fern were exactly the ones Jesus came to save, I was hit with a barrage of Scripture: "*Friendship of the world is enmity with God* (James 4:4). *Have no fellowship with the unfruitful works of darkness, but rather reprove them* (Ephesians 5:11). *What fellowship hath righteousness with unrighteousness?* (2 Corinthians 6:14)."

Trying to meet everyone's needs, let alone keep the peace, was exhausting. Exhausting and, more importantly, counterproductive. Yeshua once said seasons come and go. Clinging to one season when another arrives will eventually become destructive. The final straw came one evening at Victoria's. Because of Amber and the baby, not to mention Victoria's pool, Jacuzzi, and high-caliber snacks, hers became the place to meet and socialize—for everyone but Cowboy, who usually found some excuse to stay away and work in his shop.

As I said, we had plenty of heated discussions, but not like that night: We'd barely started before Amber was on her feet, flushed and trembling—Chip doing his best to comfort her.

"Amber, babe. Fern and me, we never—"

"You and I agreed, no more sex we said. Not 'til we're married!"

"That's right," Chip said, "'cause that's what God says."

She jabbed a finger at Fern sitting on the opposite sofa. "But it's okay for you two!?"

"Babe, I promise you, we never—"

"Men have needs, I get it. But so do women." Her voice grew thinner, higher. "And I've kept myself pure because we agreed."

"So have I." Chip started toward her, but she would have none of it.

"That's not what Mr. Rutherford says."

"What?"

"Cowboy, he's seen you two. More than once."

Chip threw a look to Fern then back to Amber. "Why would he say that?"

I glanced to Fern who stared down at her wine glass.

"Well?" Amber demanded.

"I . . ." For once Chip seemed at a loss for words. "I don't know. Rutherford . . . he's lying."

Silence fell over the group until, finally, Sophia spoke, her voice slow and husky. "That's his way."

"Lying?" I asked.

"In more ways than one," Fern muttered.

Amber turned on her. "What? What does that mean?" Fern said nothing. "Answer me!"

Fern set her glass on the coffee table and rose.

"Fern?" Chip said.

She turned and headed for the door.

"Fern?" Darlene rose to her own feet.

Without hesitation Fern opened the screen door, stepped through, and let it slap shut behind her.

"Fern!"

TWENTY-ONE

I WAS UP the rest of the night. Stars were no longer shining and the dust was so thick I occasionally had to spit. Something had to be done. Yeshua said I would know the time. And the longer I prayed, pacing and listening to the stillness, the clearer the answer. When I finally returned to my cot and squeezed in an hour of sleep before dawn, I'd reached a decision.

And, as a rookie to the silent leadings of God, I was grateful for the confirmation. No burning bushes this time. No heavenly visitations. Just another dream.

I was staggering on the deck of a ship in gale-force winds, saltwater stinging my face. It looked like a nineteenth-century schooner. Not far away stood a grizzled, gray-bearded captain in old-fashion rain gear fighting the wheel. I grabbed the closest rigging and hung on for dear life. Beside him, a young sailor in oiled raincoat and floppy hat shouted, "Captain! We can't harbor here! There are too many rocks!"

"Keep yer eyes on them lights!" the old man yelled. He motioned to the beach where three lanterns hung, swinging wildly in the wind, their eerie-green lights barely visible through the sheets of blowing water. Each was set twenty or so yards behind the other. "Line 'em up 'til there's but one!"

The dream shifted as dreams do, and suddenly I was alone on the pitching deck. The deserted wheel spun crazily as the ship tilted, turning out of control. I lunged from the rigging and managed to grab the wheel. I fought it, the spokes bruising and cutting my hands, but I eventually brought it to a stop.

When I looked up I was surprised to see my old friend, the Holy Spirit. He stood out on the bow of the ship, wind whipping his hair, enjoying the storm. And, oddly, he glowed with the same green light as the lanterns.

"What's happening?" I shouted. "I don't understand!"

He pointed to the beach which now lay far to our left.

"What?"

Again, he pointed. I squinted until I saw two of the lanterns the captain had pointed out. Lanterns, but something more. Blame it on the dream, but the first lantern was the glowing figure of Trevor Hunter. He struggled to stand against the wind while shouting into his phone. Stranger still, was the second light behind him. It was a large book, its pages open and blowing. A book I instantly sensed to be the Bible.

"Line 'em up!" the captain's voice repeated. "Line 'em up 'til there's but one!"

I fought the wheel, turning it to the left. The ship shuddered and bucked, but with effort I finally managed to point us back toward the beach. The Spirit looked over his shoulder and grinned while motioning for me to continue. I did my best, sometimes overcompensating too far to the left, then too far to the right. But eventually, for the most part, I was able to line up the two lights. Actually, three. Because when they were perfectly aligned, the Holy Spirit's glow made up the third. All three lights became one—Trevor on his phone, the open Scriptures, and the Holy Spirit.

The wind, waves, and the violent pitching suddenly stopped. I opened my eyes. I blinked at the light of the rising sun illuminating my ceiling. The dream was over. And so was any trace of confusion. I would call Trevor. What Yeshua had planned after that was anybody's guess. But that was a habit I'd grown used to.

೧

The call to Trevor went pretty much as expected—except for the unexpected wrinkle.

"That's fantastic!" he said. "The governor will be so pleased."

"I'm still not sure what he hopes to accomplish."

"Just communication, Will. Opening the lines of communication so we can find a win/win for us all."

He still thought he could negotiate with God, but I let it go. "You'll make the reservations for Chip and me to fly out of Vegas?" I asked. "Give us a day or two to pack and drive back there?"

"Actually, things have heated up a bit. In more ways than one."

"Meaning?"

"Have you ever been to Washington?"

"I live there, remember?"

"No, dude. D.C., Washington, D.C. The governor has moved our operations there."

"Trevor—"

"No worries, man. You'll love it."

I closed my eyes and breathed deeply. *Now what are you up to?* I silently prayed.

But, of course, there was no answer. Actually, there was always an answer. It's just Yeshua seldom bothered to share it—at least with me. "Because," as he frequently pointed out, "you'll just mess things up trying to help."

"It's still going to take a day to drive to Las Vegas and catch a flight," I said.

"Actually not."

"Meaning?"

"We'll chopper you out of there before nightfall."

"A helicopter?"

"Just to Nellis Air Force Base where a plane will be waiting."

TWENTY-TWO

WITH SO FEW clothes to pack, I was ready within an hour. It was more difficult for Chip with his multiple pants, shorts, shirts, shoes, electronic gizmos, and, of course, various toiletries. I know I'm old-school, but I had no idea men needed so many hair products.

Packing was easy. Leaving the group was hard. In the short amount of time, I'd really grown to care for these people. Yes, it was my first experience with church and I'm sure my glasses were a bit rose-colored, but if this was what Yeshua meant about experiencing a community of believers, sign me up. Granted, Cowboy's rock tumbler analogy came to mind more times than I could count, and it took a bit of imagination to picture them as polished gems. But if Yeshua's reason for my visit was to fast-track my heart into loving his people, I'd been in the express lane.

The helicopter's thumping could be heard for miles and gave everyone time to step outside and say goodbye.

"You okay?" Darlene asked.

"Yeah," I said. "It's just saying goodbye is tougher than I thought."

"Who said anything about saying goodbye?"

I cocked my head at her as the others arrived, circling around us.

"We took a vote," she said. "We're driving back there to meet you."

"You're what?"

"Somebody has to look out for you," Amber said as she set Billie-Jean on the ground.

"You're driving back?" I repeated.

"They're dropping off the Starliner tomorrow," Victoria said.

"Starliner?"

"Top of the line motor home. If we're traveling together, we're traveling in style."

I turned to the others. "All of you?"

"'Cept Rutherford," Sophia said. "Somebody has to mind the place."

"He volunteered?"

"Not exactly."

The group traded looks. Darlene paraphrased a quote from somewhere in Titus.

"Now you're quoting the Bible?" I asked.

Before she could answer, Victoria produced one of the balloons she'd ordered and placed it in my palm. "I thought you might want this," she said. I looked down at it, felt my throat tightening. "Don't forget to inflate it," she said. "It's no good if it's not inflated."

I looked up and quietly said, "Thank you."

Before I could respond, she stepped in and gave me a hug. "No, pastor. Thank you."

"There it is!" Chip pointed to the helicopter appearing through the thick haze.

As we watched, Sophia slipped a small, rainbow pouch into my hand.

"What's this?" I asked.

"Jade. The best crystal for luck and protection."

"Sophia . . ."

"I know, I know. But it's shaped like a cross so you can play all the angles." I gave her a look. She shrugged and added, "At least it'll keep the vampires away."

The helicopter, large and blue and white, touched down over fifty yards away—no doubt to spare us from its own man-made sandstorm.

"Goodbye, Uncle Will!" Amber was the second person to throw her arms around me—a full-on embrace, the first as I recall.

"Bye-bye," Billie-Jean yelled.

I bent down and scooped her up. "Bye-bye, little one." I pushed aside her bangs and kissed her forehead. "I'll see you soon."

"Bye-bye," she repeated. "Bye-bye."

I gave her another kiss and handed her over to Amber when the cloud of chopper dust finally arrived, forcing us to turn our heads. As we did, Fern stepped closer. She was in no mood for a hug and I didn't offer one. Instead, she spoke just loud enough for me to hear over the helicopter's roar.

"I'm praying," she said.

I smiled. "That's great."

She shook her head. "For you. I'm praying for you."

Before I could respond, she looked away and stepped back to join the others.

Chip, finishing his own goodbyes with Amber, motioned to the helicopter, its door open, the stairs unfolding. "We better get going!"

I nodded and turned to Darlene a final time. "Thank you," I said.

"For what?"

I didn't know where to start. She saved me the effort by giving me a quick kiss on the cheek. Startled, I found myself trying to return it, which only made us look (and feel) like a couple clumsy teenagers.

She pulled back, regaining her composure. "For luck," she explained.

"Right," I said, smiling at her fluster. "For luck."

"Will?"

I nodded and replied, "Shutting up now."

Chip picked up his bags and started forward. "Come on, let's go!"

As Darlene brushed the hair from her face, I thought of finishing off with something clever, but knew better. Instead, I simply said, "See you soon." And she nodded.

After another round of goodbyes, including Amber's and Chip's shouted exchanges—"I love you, babe! I love you more! I love you most!"—we ducked our heads into the blowing sand and approached the chopper. As we arrived and stepped up into the cabin I hoped, I prayed we'd see each other soon. But, taking my seat and looking back at them through the tinted window, I knew sometimes prayers aren't always answered the way we expect—or want.

PART THREE

CHAPTER
TWENTY-THREE

WE'D BARELY STEPPED from the helicopter at Nellis Air Force Base before we were greeted by a man and woman in suits who hustled us onto a private jet. I'd never been on one—not the usual mode of transport for ex-college professors turned public pariah. Plush carpet, recessed lighting, leather seats (actually, recliners), deeply polished walnut, and more than enough leg space. All it lacked were peanuts and an inflight movie.

No problem for Chip, as he always had a stash of junk food, and his computer was filled with unlimited entertainment. We were barely in the air when the cabin was filled with the stench of corn chips as he began watching his first movie. I tried not to look, catching only glimpses of the spurting blood and naked lovers. A year ago I would barely be fazed, but now—after all these months detoxifying from our culture, I'd forgotten how rapidly things had decayed. What's the old proverb about putting a frog in a pot of water? He doesn't feel a thing as you gradually turn up the heat until he's boiled to death. I'm not sure of the science behind that, but it's a good analogy.

No wonder Yeshua's heart was breaking. Everyone was calling the drought God's wrath. Maybe it was. Or maybe it was his urgent cry for us to stop and come to our senses. I turned to Chip, ready to say something, but he'd fallen asleep, already bored with the depravity on the screen.

The view outside was less discouraging, but not by much. It was summer. The fields below should be green and bursting with life. Instead, what I saw through a thick haze was the dead, brown bleakness of what looked like winter.

It was 1:35 a.m. when we arrived at the Ronald Reagan Washington National Airport. We taxied to a special terminal for special flights and there to meet us was . . .

"Hey, dudes, welcome to Washington."

I turned to see Trevor's assistant, Pug. At least I thought it was Pug. He had the same perma-grin. But he'd traded his cargo shorts and flip-flops in for a suit and tie. And his long, blonde hair was trimmed into something grown-up. He threw his arms around me into one of those half-hug, jock things. He tried the same with Chip, but the kid held him off with a more formal handshake. Old memories die hard.

Turning back to me, he said, "Bet you got a ton of questions, right?"

I nodded. "You could say that."

"Right. We got lots to cover and like zero time, so I'll fill you in on the ride."

The ride was a black SUV with dark, tinted windows—just the thing for sightseeing at night. And the fill-you-in part? "So, the governor, he's making Trevor his running mate, I mean no surprise, right? Both hot-looking dudes. The assassination of Trev's wife was a real bonding thing. And his popularity with the kids, he's gonna be a slam dunk for the woke Christian vote?"

"Woke Christian?" I asked.

"Catchy, huh? Trev's idea."

Turning from the window, Chip asked. "And he's brought me and Will in because . . . ?"

"To get on top of this whole wrath/drought thing."

"On top?" I asked.

"Tell the governor what he has to do to bring it to an end."

I frowned. "Why the governor?"

"For votes," Chip said. "If he's the man who ends the drought then—"

Pug finished, "—he's the man to run the country."

I sat back in my seat, not surprised, but not thrilled with what I was hearing.

"Why all the rush?" Chip asked. "The elections aren't 'til November."

"He's addressing the country with a major policy position this week."

"What day?" I asked.

"That's up to you. The sooner you two reach an agreement, the sooner he can make the announcement."

"And be the nation's hero." There was no missing Chip's sarcasm.

Pug countered, "And stop all this needless suffering."

"I'm not sure it's entirely needless," I said.

"Whatever. Let's get you two settled and get some rest. Big day tomorrow. And maybe, no promises, if we got time, there's somebody in the Oval Office who might want to say hi."

My jaw slacked. I'd like to tell you what was running through my head, but at the moment it was too noisy inside for even me to know. Things got no better when we pulled up to the Jefferson Intercontinental Hotel—a modern edifice of steel and glass illuminating the night sky. Pug opened the door, signaled the porter, a young woman, and ordered, "Penthouse."

She replied in a thick Latin accent. "Yes, sir."

"Penthouse?" I asked.

"Governor Proctor feels it's the least he can do."

"Pug, listen," I said. "It's like I told Trevor, I really don't know what I'm supposed to say to him. What I'm supposed to do."

"You'll figure it out."

"But—"

"Love to talk, big guy, but I gotta jet. Monster day, tomorrow." He stepped back into the SUV. "They'll take care of you—room service, anything. Just ask, we got you covered."

"Pug—"

"Pick you up 7:15 tomorrow." He gave me a thumbs-up and shut the door.

The porter, who loaded her cart with Chip's back-packs and suitcase, said, "If you'll follow me, please."

"Here," Chip moved in to help. "I can get that."

"Please, sir. It is my job."

He nodded and we followed her to the doors. They hissed open and we stepped into a bright lobby of white marble, black leather sofas, and glass tables. We passed the receptionist and headed for the elevators.

"Shouldn't we check in?" I asked.

"It has already been handled," the porter said. We arrived at the elevators, and she pressed the button. While waiting, she turned to us and half-whispered, "You are the prophet, yes?"

"I, uh, that's not really—"

"How did you know?" Chip asked.

Still keeping her voice low, she answered. "My group, we have been praying for you these many months."

Chip and I traded looks.

"Group?" I asked.

"There are four of us. We meet on the rooftop in the evenings.

The elevator doors opened just as the lights flickered out. Bright emergency lights immediately flooded the lobby.

"What's going on?" Chip asked.

"Rolling blackouts," the porter said. "If you follow me, we will take the stairs. When the power returns, I shall deliver your luggage by the elevator." She turned and started for the steps.

Somehow, by the grace of God, I made it up all fourteen flights without any help of a defibrillator.

TWENTY-FOUR

DESPITE THE THREE-HOUR time difference, I was up at 4:30 the next morning praying. I pleaded with Yeshua to tell me what to do, what to say. And for my efforts I got . . . nothing. Or maybe I did and just didn't know it—which seems to be one of his favorite ways of communication. I even played a little Bible roulette, flipping back and forth through the pages, waiting for something to leap out at me. Again, nothing.

I remembered the last book in the Bible, the Revelation. It was full of so many plagues, signs, and judgments that I figured as a "prophet" I should read up on them. But by the time I got to the eighth chapter my head was swimming with so many angels and trumpets and seals I figured I'd leave any and all explanations to the theologians—unless, of course, there was a Dr. Seuss version with pictures and rhyme.

Of course I was fascinated by Yeshua's own appearance to the disciple, John. Seems even his best friends did face plants when he showed up in all his glory. (Note to self: Straighten up and stop being so snarky when addressing the King of the Universe.)

The letters to the seven churches were also interesting, particularly the one to Laodicea which sounded uncomfortably familiar:

"You say, 'I am rich; I have acquired wealth and do not need a thing.' But you do not realize that you are wretched, pitiful, poor, blind and naked."

There was more, but I got the point.

The trip to Governor Proctor's office was memorable. I'd never been to Washington, D.C., and catching glimpses of the Washington Monument and other landmarks between business buildings was impressive, almost surreal.

"What about last night's power outage?" Chip asked Pug as we rode. "Did it hit the whole city?"

"Yeah, mostly," Pug said. "They've been having rolling blackouts like a couple months now."

"Because of the drought?" I asked

"Yeah. D.C. doesn't use hydroelectric power, but they need water to cool their other sources."

"Sources?"

"Gas and nuclear."

I looked back out the window. The drought was having an impact beyond what I could have ever imagined.

Ten minutes later we slowed and turned into an underground parking structure. "Here we are," Pug said.

I glanced over to Chip who was wrinkling his nose. "What's wrong?" I asked.

"That rotten egg smell."

I sniffed the air. He was right, there was something, but I only caught a trace of it.

"It's terrible," he said. "Like back at Malibu." He raised his hand to cover his nose and mouth. "Can't you smell it?"

"A little."

What's that?" Pug asked.

"That smell."

Pug breathed in then shook his head while Chip pulled his shirt up over his nose and mouth. "You okay, little dude?" he asked.

"Yeah," Chip said. He lowered his shirt, trying to be cool. "It's nothing."

But it was something. I could tell by the way his eyes watered. And by the time the SUV pulled to a stop and we stepped out into the garage, he looked terribly pale.

"You sure you're okay?" I asked as we started for the elevators.

He nodded, paused, then bent over, and vomited.

"Dude," Pug stepped back, checking his shoes for splatter.

"Sorry." Chip rose and wiped his mouth.

"What's going on?" Pug asked.

"It's that smell."

"I don't smell anything."

"It's—" Chip shook his head. "It's nothing. I'm fine." We resumed our walk to the elevators.

"You sure you're okay?" I repeated.

He nodded. But we no sooner arrived before he hurled again.

Pug and I traded looks.

"Maybe we better cancel," I said. "Come back when you're—"

"No." Chip said. "No, it's just something—" Again he retched.

"Chip?"

The elevator door rattled open and he waved us in. "Go ahead without me."

"Not if you're—"

"I'll catch up. I just need a sec."

"You want to go back to the hotel?" Pug asked.

"No, I—" Chip stopped then swallowed hard. "Yeah," he said, "that'd be cool."

I turned to Pug. "Tell the governor we'll postpone. Maybe tomorrow when he's—"

"No," Chip shook his head. "You guys go ahead."

"Not if you're feeling—"

"I'll head back to the hotel. It's nothing."

"Chip . . ."

"I'll be fine. Go."

I looked to Pug who held the elevator, its door bucking against his hand. "I can call a doctor," he said. "Send him over to check you out."

"I don't need a—"

"Okay, that sounds good," I said. I turned to Chip "We'll go without you, but only if you promise to let the doctor see you."

"Will . . ."

I shook my head, holding my ground.

"Alright, fine. Call the stupid doctor, but I'm fine." How many times do I have to say it? I'm fine."

Pug pulled out his phone and began dialing.

"Fine," I said. "Do that and we'll be fine. Okay?"

"Fine!"

CHAPTER
TWENTY-FIVE

"REVEREND THOMAS." THE secretary, a petite blonde, was on her feet before we finished entering. The reception area was small, with white sheers, blue colonial drapes, and the feel of American history.

I cleared my throat. "I'm really, not a—"

"He likes to keep it informal, right, Will?"

I turned and saw Trevor rising from a red and green tartan sofa.

"Uh, right," I said as we shook hands.

"Good to see you." He turned to Pug. "Thanks, man."

"No prob," Pug said. "Need anything else?"

"We're good."

Pug gave a quick glance to the governor's closed door. "You sure? 'Cause I can hang here 'til—"

"We're good, Pug."

"Right, cool." He nodded and headed for the exit. "Call when you need me."

"Thanks, man." Turning back to me, Trevor said, "Really glad you could make it, Will. We've got some big plans and it would be super if you joined us in the announcement."

"Announcement?" I asked.

He grinned. "You'll see." Looking over to the secretary, he asked, "Can we go in?"

"He's waiting."

"Thanks, Bri." By the way they traded smiles I could tell they had a past. And maybe a present. He knocked lightly on the door, paused, then opened it. That's when the screaming began.

Proctor's desk was ten feet away. On it, shadowy forms, twelve to eighteen inches high, shrieked and staggered. They were identical to the ones I had seen in Malibu and later in Vegas. The same amphibian faces, oozing lesions and razor-sharp talons. Exactly the same and equally frightening. I spun to Trevor, then Proctor. Neither saw nor heard as the governor rose from his desk to greet us.

"Will, so good to see you again."

I glanced back to the reception area. Running out the office screaming in terror was not the first impression I wanted to make, but this . . .

"Please, come, come." He motioned us inside. As Trevor closed the door, I quickly scanned the room, hoping to see Yeshua or the Spirit. I'd even settle for my glow-in-the-dark military escort. None were present. At least from what I saw. More pleasantries were exchanged and I tried being cordial, though it's difficult being cordial when facing the demons of hell. As I approached his desk, the creatures backed away from me, huddling closer and closer to one another. Apparently, they weren't the only ones afraid. By the time I eased myself into one of the two armchairs in front of the desk, they'd condensed into a thick, black cloud.

As Proctor sat, I stole another look around the room. Still no sign of reinforcements. I turned back to Proctor as the cloud morphed into the head of a giant snake and slowly rose off the desk. I could only stare as it floated along the man's chest, then his neck and, for the briefest second, covered his face before it was gone.

"I can't tell you how grateful we are that you found time to join us."

I blinked. Proctor remained smiling. "Yes, well," I cleared my throat, "Trevor can be persuasive."

He turned his smile on Trevor. "He's an invaluable member of the team." Trevor practically glowed. "He was the first to apprise me of this wrath business; God calling down judgment. Do you think it's true, that we're really experiencing the 'wrath of God'?"

I thought of playing it safe, enjoying the good ol' days where Will Thomas could claim ignorance. But those days had come and gone. "Yes," I said, careful to keep my voice even. "I believe this is the Lord's way of getting our attention, of calling our country to repent of its evil."

Proctor raised his hands, placing fingertip to fingertip. "Evil. That's, well that's a very strong word."

I swallowed.

He continued. "Sadly, I would have to agree." Turning to Trevor he added, "We agree."

Trevor nodded. "Absolutely."

Proctor turned to the credenza behind him and retrieved a folder. "That's why I've taken great pains to draw this up." He turned back to me, holding the file in his hands. "It's a proclamation. My proposed plans should the people of this great nation choose me to become their leader." He handed them to me. "I wanted you to look at this. Review them, before I go public. And, if you agree, consider endorsing them."

"Endorsing them?" I asked.

He motioned to the folder. "Please, read."

I opened the folder. There were a good two or three dozen pages.

"No need to read it all," he said. "I believe you'll recognize the bullet points."

I nodded, found the first, and silently read. *Don't commit adultery.* Then the second, *Don't bear false witness.* And the third, *Honor your father and mother.* Looking up, I said, "These are the Ten Commandments."

"In part, yes."

"I don't understand. What do you mean, you'll be 'announcing' these?"

"As my commitment to the American people."

I stared back at the folder then frowned. "This is all very impressive, but . . ."

"But?"

"It seems to me another nation tried this once."

He chuckled. "The ancient nation of Israel, yes. And, I might point out, with great success. Until modern-day mores refused to follow them. Until we began treating them as outdated suggestions."

"They're the Ten Commandments," Trevor said. "Not the Ten Suggestions."

"Is this," my frown deepened, "is this something you'd try to enforce, to turn into law?"

Proctor gave another chuckle. "Law? Hardly. In this country, we can barely agree on the law of gravity. No. But I would put these principles back into the forefront of our nation's consciousness. I'd look for ways to encourage their obedience. Provide incentives. Perhaps tax breaks for those who choose to follow."

Trevor added, "Nothing gets people's attention like their pocketbooks."

Proctor agreed. "There are a thousand ways to enforce policy without turning it into law. At least in the beginning."

"In the beginning?" I asked.

He simply smiled.

I looked back down at the document. "This is . . . impressive."

"It's God's Holy Word, it should be."

My mind raced. Was something like this possible? After all, they are God's commands. His Law. And if we took them seriously, if we took him seriously . . . I looked back up and asked, "What about separation of church and state? Wouldn't something like this be political suicide?"

Trevor answered, "It might have been, before. But now . . . not if people are serious about stopping the drought, putting an end to the pain and suffering."

Proctor continued. "Some will resist, of course, at least in the beginning. But if they continue to refuse . . . well, who do you suppose the public will turn against if the pain and suffering continues?"

I looked back down and read, "Remember the Sabbath day and keep it holy."

Proctor explained, "We'll reintroduce the Blue Laws. States have had them for years. We'll encourage people to take Sundays off. Create incentives for them to attend the church of their choice."

"What about the Jews?" I asked. "They meet on Saturdays."

"They'll adjust."

"And other faiths . . . Muslims, Buddhists? What about atheists?"

The governor answered slowly and carefully, "They'll have to make some very hard decisions."

I turned back to the paper.

"So what do you think?" Trevor asked. "Is this something you can get behind?"

I raised my eyebrows. "It all sounds good." Silence filled the room as I continued to read. After several moments Proctor's intercom buzzed. He reached for it and answered, "Yes?"

"The car is waiting for your 8:30 with Senator Hutton."

"I'll be right there." Proctor looked back to me. "Take your time, study it. Then get back to me." I slowly nodded. "But Will?" I looked up. "Do it quickly. I'm making the announcement tomorrow night."

Trevor continued, "With a giant rally the following day. At the Lincoln Memorial."

I turned to him. "The Lincoln Memorial?"

He grinned. "Fitting, don't you think?"

CHAPTER
TWENTY-SIX

TO SAY MY mind spun was an understatement. Before me was a clear opportunity to turn the country back to God. Isn't that what Yeshua wanted? But Proctor? Those creatures? Still, everything he said was biblical. The Ten Commandments. What better foundation. Would people protest? Of course. No one likes to be told what to do. But we're talking about God's, holy commands.

My confusion only worsened when we headed back down to the parking garage and the elevator door rattled open to reveal three reporters hovering around our SUV. Pug muttered a couple oaths (and I thought them) as we stepped out to immediately become raw hamburger in a shark tank—the recorders raised, the voices shouting:

"What solution did you and Governor Proctor reach? Are you calling off the drought? What do you say to those whose livelihoods you've destroyed? How does it feel to shipwreck the entire economy?"

Things were not much better outside the hotel, though I was grateful for the two security guys, just slightly smaller than Mount Rushmore, who appeared and escorted me through the crowd.

Chip appeared to have recovered from his nausea, as evident by the stack of room service trays piled outside our room. When I entered, he was sitting on his bed, finishing off a BLT, and talking on his phone. He motioned to the muted TV and I saw my parking garage press conference in all its seventy-two-inch diagonal glory.

"Are you kidding me?" I grumbled. "That was just thirty minutes ago."

"Shh." Chip motioned to his phone. I dropped into the nearest chair doing my best not to fall into one of the old, Will Thomas, self-pitying sulks. Meanwhile, Chip was in deep conversation. "Uh-huh . . . Okay . . ." He paused. "Right . . . Uh-huh . . . No, I hear you . . ." He paused again. "Okay." Another pause. "Okay." I had little doubt who was on the other end. When it came to idle chatter and opinions about everything, he'd met his match with Amber. "Uh-huh . . . Okay . . ." I looked back to the TV, now displaying my escorted entrance into the hotel, followed by what looked like man-on-the-street interviews—as the crowd continued to grow.

And that pretty much summed up the rest of my day—listening to Chip's side of Amber's frequent calls describing what city they just passed, what they had for lunch, who was making who crazy, what cute little thing Billie-Jean was doing, then always ending with the proverbial, "You hang up. No, you hang up. No, you. No, you. Have you hung up yet?"

Later, because no one recognized him, Chip had the freedom to roam the streets and visit some of the historical landmarks. This gave me plenty of time to plead with Yeshua for some clear-cut, Is-It-Door-A-or-Door-B? answers. Of course it wasn't his style, but I figured it wouldn't hurt to ask. When all else failed, I finally got around to the Bible. And what an eye-opener. It seemed every time God clearly laid down the law to his people, they repented . . . for a while. Then he laid it down again and they repented. And again. It was an endless cycle of "wash, rinse, and repeat." No matter how many times he stressed obedience and underlined the consequences of disobedience, they disobeyed. It was disappointing to say the least. The hours of study and confinement took their toll, spiritually and emotionally. Unable to leave the room. Afraid to go out. Was this what it was like to suffer imprisonment for Christ—well, except for the A.C., twenty-four-hour room service, and 480 thread count sheets?

It was late evening when Chip finally returned. He'd just spoken to the young porter we'd met the night before and, in spite of my resistance, dragged me to the rooftop to meet her little prayer group. There were only four: Luciana, the porter, Maryam, and Bijan who worked in housekeeping, and David from hospitality who was confined to a wheelchair. The view, what we saw of it through the thick haze, was not magnificent, mostly shadowy rooftops with air ducts and satellite dishes. Although, in the distance, you could see the White House and American flag, the floodlights making them glow like beacons in the dark.

"Thanks for letting us pray with you," David said. His voice was thin with a faint lisp.

Luciana added, "It is a great honor."

"No," I said, "the honor is ours."

"Just you four?" Chip asked.

"Yeah," David said. He turned to the others. "But we're a tenacious bunch, right guys?" They smiled. He added, "And there are others like us around the country."

"Many," Luciana said.

"You guys know about tomorrow's announcement?" Chip asked.

"Of course," David said. "You are the angel we have been waiting for."

"Sent from God," Luciana agreed.

I shot an alarmed look to Chip. "Um, listen," I said. "I don't know what you're thinking, and we sure don't want to disappoint you, but I'm no angel."

Chip chuckled, "You got that right."

"But you are the angel," Luciana insisted, "the one spoken of in the Bible."

Seeing the concern on my face, David laughed. "No, no, no. We aren't talking about that kind of angel." I relaxed slightly as he continued. "In the Bible the word *angel* can simply mean *messenger*."

Bijan added with a grin, "No wings necessary."

"You are the messenger," Luciana said. "To the church." I wasn't exactly sure I felt any better. But before I could respond, she asked, "May we put our hands on you?"

"Um . . ."

Chip jumped in. "Sure. He has no problem with that."

"And you too?" she asked.

Now it was Chip's turn to hesitate. "Yeah . . . sure."

Bijan and Maryam produced two, frayed, lawn chairs, probably used for rooftop sunning.

"Please," David motioned for us to sit.

Chip and I stole quick looks then eased ourselves into the chairs as the others gathered around.

David began. Others joined in, quietly worshipping God. Eventually they got around to us, praying we would be instruments for "his kingdom to come." The phrase startled me. It was exactly how Yeshua taught me to pray when we were battling over Billie-Jean's heart ailment. And there was more. Just as Yeshua instructed, they asked that as his kingdom grew inside us it would spill out onto the world so "his will would be done . . . on earth just as it is in heaven." Despite the time and our differences, the prayer was amazingly similar.

And yet, there was no surge of power, no blinding flash of insight. (A clear yes or no over my decision wouldn't hurt, either.) I felt nothing except encouragement that four people thought enough about us to pray. And pray they did. Often times returning to quiet praise and adoration. It seemed to last forever, and I didn't blame Chip for occasionally shifting and glancing around. I did the same; opening my eyes, hoping for some audio-visual aid. I even lifted my head and craned my neck to steal a peek across the rooftops to the White House. And that's when I spotted them. Somehow, despite the distance, they were in closeup; figures I knew very well—the ones I'd first encountered in my hospital room, and later when they wielded their weapons to protect me in Malibu and Las Vegas, and still later, on the bus heading into the desert. They encircled the building, not moving but standing stoically on guard. And, as our little group prayed, others appeared, some smaller, some larger, filling every conceivable gap, creating an impregnable wall. Because, directly in front of them, on every side was the hissing and shrieking cloud of blackness I'd seen so many times before.

I blinked and was suddenly back in my chair, looking up to the four praying over us. Four common, everyday people. The type you would never notice on the street. Only four holding back the forces of hell. And yet, even then I knew they were in the majority.

TWENTY-SEVEN

FOR WHAT IT was worth, I had another restless night. We got hit with another rolling blackout that left no sound in the room save Chip's snoring. Despite my prayers and study and, yes, whining (as I've said, some habits die hard), by sunrise I still had no answer for Proctor. I thought of my recent dream about making decisions—the three guiding lights: Scripture, the Holy Spirit, and circumstances. I suppose a fourth could be godly council. What I wouldn't give for a deep, meaningful conversation. Staring over at Chip, his mouth gaping, I wasn't convinced I had it.

Until I heard knocking at the door.

"Dr. Thomas?"

I glanced to the radio alarm. Still no display thanks to the power outage.

More knocking. "Dr. Thomas. This is Luciana. From the prayer group?"

"Luciana?"

"Good morning, sir. A woman, she refuses to leave the lobby. She insists she knows you."

"A woman?"

"And her dog. His name is Siggy."

I was on my feet in a shot. I passed the mirror, spending an extra moment or two . . . or three. After a sniff test, I threw on my polo shirt. Grabbing Chip's sunglasses and his Mariner's baseball cap, should any paparazzi be up this time of morning, I raced to the elevator. I waited for its arrival, cursing the slowness, "Come on, come on!" until I remembered there was no power. I turned and raced down the stairs, all fourteen flights, slipping and catching myself more than once. I reached the lobby level, took a moment to catch my breath, then threw open the door to see . . . Patricia in all her fashion-model beauty. Our embrace was as awkward as always—me unsure the appropriate amount of pressure to apply, she adjusting her bony frame to accommodate.

As we separated, she greeted me with social skills that had not improved over the year. "You look terrible. You're way too skinny." While, under the scowls of the hotel staff, Siggy barked and leaped with such excitement he sent me staggering. "Okay, boy, I missed you too, okay, okay . . ."

I invited her up to the room for breakfast. But after reminding me "Christians must avoid even the appearance of evil," and remembering how close I came to death the last time I climbed all those stairs, we voted for the hotel restaurant, until they made it clear no animals were allowed—not even emotional support dogs for world-famous prophets. We settled, instead, for a long walk, my cap pulled low to avoid any recognition. This didn't stop my phone from buzzing as it had a dozen times yesterday and started up fresh and alive this morning. There was no doubt who the caller was and no doubt I'd avoid him until I reached my decision.

"So," Patricia said as we walked along the street, "you've become quite the celebrity."

"Not by choice," I said.

"I know, I've been praying." I turned to her. More quietly she added, "Every day."

We walked for what seemed hours and, with her prodding, I downloaded the year's headlines. I was surprised that except for my months of desert solitude, she already knew the worst.

"As I mentioned," she said, "you've become quite the celebrity."

Feeling guilty for monopolizing the conversation, I asked, "What about you? It's been over a year. How have you been?"

"Everything is the same," she said, "except for the people and reporters who keep asking for details of our life together."

The phrase "life together" caught me off guard and buoyed my spirits.

"Of course, I must constantly make it plain there is nothing special between us, that we are simply friends."

"Right, right," I said, "just friends." Unable to leave well enough alone, I added, "And yet, here you are, flying all the way across the country to visit me." She stared hard at the sidewalk, giving me time to fall back and regroup. "To bring Siggy, I mean." I reached down and patted him. "Good boy. Good Siggy."

She remained silent.

I quickly pivoted. "So, where are you staying? For how long?"

"My layover is eighteen hours."

"Layover?"

"I am returning to Papua New Guinea, to the mission field."

"Really." I cleared my throat, hiding the disappointment. Somehow, I always figured we'd get together. Eventually. So many signs pointed to it. Except the one that said she was way out of my league. "Why exactly are you leaving?" I asked.

"In Papua New Guinea, the people are still hungry for God."

"And not here in the States?"

"Here we have become inoculated."

"Inoculated?"

"In medicine, to vaccinate, we introduce an imitation of the very virus we are trying to prevent. This allows the patient's system to build immunity to the actual disease."

"And we're doing that here?"

"The gospel presented here is often an imitation, so watered down it prevents the true gospel from taking hold."

I was always impressed by Patricia's bluntness. Small talk was a skill she never quite developed. For most it was off-putting, for me it was refreshing and one of the many things I admired. "You don't think we have much of a chance to change?" I asked.

"If this drought is truly God's wrath, and I believe you when you say it is, what good has it accomplished?"

"Not much," I agreed. "Not yet."

"I'm afraid you are right."

We walked several moments in silence, which was fine; I needed time to readjust to the fact she would be gone again. We agreed to see some of the sights and, after paying a hefty fee (i.e., tip) for Siggy to ride along, we caught a cab to the Lincoln Memorial. The view from the top of its steps was awesome. The long reflecting pool stretching over six hundred yards to the Washington Monument, inspiring. Little wonder this was the place Martin Luther King Jr. chose to deliver his "I Have a

Dream" speech—and where Proctor, in his infinite ego, would hold tomorrow's rally. Inside, the memorial was equally impressive with its towering pillars, marble floor, and the giant statue of the man sitting deep in thought. It was there, under his solemn gaze, that I finally laid out to Patricia the details of my dilemma.

"So," she said, after I finished, "if you say yes, you may actually bring the country back to God."

I nodded. "By insisting we follow the Ten Commandments."

"And that is a problem, following God's law?"

"It is, if it doesn't last. Then there's the whole issue of trusting the man proposing it."

"The governor."

"Yes."

"The Lord can accomplish his will with anyone, can he not? Even through the mouth of a jackass."

"Balaam's donkey?"

She smiled. "You have been studying your Bible."

"But," I argued, "Satan can use Scripture too."

"You're referring to Christ's temptation in the wilderness."

"Yes."

She had no answer and we both fell silent, looking out over the reflecting pool.

Finally, I continued, "Then there's the whole free will thing, God doesn't force people to worship him.

That's their decision. And if we try to outdo him and strongarm them—"

She completed my thought, "It could tear the country apart."

"Precisely. So, you see my problem."

She nodded. "You either agree with a man whose methods you do not trust to draw our country back to God. Or you disagree with him knowing God will most likely continue his judgment."

"Yes."

"That's quite a predicament you've gotten yourself into, Will Thomas."

I sighed. "Just like old times." I shook my head. "Why would God put me in an impossible situation?"

"Perhaps he trusts you."

I looked up, startled.

"I don't understand all that is happening, Will. But . . . I believe he has chosen the correct man."

"You do?"

"And I believe I may have an answer." I waited as she looked up at the statue of Lincoln towering over us. "In some ways, wasn't his dilemma similar to yours? If he ordered the slaves to be free, it could tear the country apart. If he ignored the problem, the human bondage would continue."

I stared up at his face, so solemn and troubled. "How did he reach his decision?"

"Prayer." I looked back to her and she continued. "I've read in the beginning he was not much of a Christian, more of a skeptic and moralist. But as the pressures built, he turned more often to prayer."

"Pressure does that to a person."

"Yes."

"But I have been praying."

"And the changes I see in you prove it."

I brushed off the compliment. "So what do you suggest?"

"Just one thing."

"Which is . . . ?"

"Pray more."

Once we found a taxi that would take Siggy, we drove to Patricia's hotel. I suggested dinner, but she declined, saying she had an early flight. When I offered to accompany her to the airport, she agreed, although reluctantly. I suspected the reason. She wasn't fond of public displays of affection and saying goodbye to me in the airport would be as hard on her as it would be on me. At least that's what I hoped.

I dropped her off, just a mere six blocks away which, in D.C. terms could be a good mile or two, and decided to walk home. Walk and, yes, quietly pray. Though, quietly did not exactly happen. A buzz was growing on the sidewalks outside the restaurants and bars I passed.

Proctor had made his announcement. Apparently, sides were quickly forming.

"He can't do that!" a thirtysomething business-woman argued with colleagues waiting outside for a table.

"How else are we going to stop the drought?" a second asked.

"I see no connection," she countered.

"Then you're not paying attention."

A third weighed in. "What if that prophet guy is right? What's wrong with getting us back on track?"

"What's wrong with keeping your religion out of my face?"

I pulled down my cap, lowered my head, and jock-eyed inside to look at one of the TV monitors. Everyone around me had an opinion, many heated, and so loud it was hard for me to hear. Sadly, it wasn't necessary. Up on the screen was a photo of Proctor and me shaking hands. The best I figured it was either AI or from our meeting in Las Vegas. Either way, the point was clear. I no longer had to make the decision. It was made for me.

CHAPTER
TWENTY-EIGHT

IT WAS A lot harder getting back into the hotel than getting out. I spotted the crowd a hundred yards away. Good news travels fast. There were no signs or placards yet, though I suspected they'd come soon enough. And, despite the baseball cap and sunglasses, let alone security guards, there was no way I'd approach and risk being recognized. With Siggy at my side I circled the building, giving the crowd a wide berth. There had to be some sort of service entrance or loading dock. I found both on the backside. I climbed the half dozen steps to a metal door and tried it. Locked. I knocked. Then banged. No answer. I finally pulled out my phone and called Chip.

"Uncle Will," he answered.

"Chip, I—"

"You won't believe it, but you're really pissing a lot of people off."

"Right. Listen, I—"

"You're all over the news. And the crowd outside the hotel? Awesome!"

"I'm at the service entrance and I—"

"Well, you better get in here before someone recognizes you 'cause it could get real—"

"Chip!"

"What?"

"It's locked. I need you to come down and let me in."

"Well why didn't you say so. I'm on it."

He was right, of course. We were all over the news. But not everyone was angry. It depended on what network they watched. On one the commentator called us:

"The sword of God, folks. It's double-edged just like in the Bible. The prophet's promise of wrath and destruction or the governor's solution of hope and mercy."

While another channel insisted we were:

"No better than the extremist leaders of Islamic states; demanding you live under Sharia Law or face the consequences."

But both sides agreed on one thing. What was supposed to be a small rally tomorrow at the Lincoln Memorial would be a lot larger. Already, the D.C. police were making plans while the National Guard had been put on alert. It would be a massive rally of both supporters and protesters. Still, despite Trevor's multiple calls, I did my best to avoid answering—until my last and final visit with Yeshua.

It was another, near sleepless night. Despite strict orders, Siggy lay stretched out on the bed beside me, competing with Chip in the Olympic snoring event. With little to do except occasionally drift off to sleep where I dreamed I wasn't sleeping (which is as bad as not sleeping), I thought I'd catch up on a little journal writing. Not that it would be much good since everything was buried somewhere back in the desert. But the events and the changes still happening in me should probably be recorded. I couldn't explain them all, but people should know. Regardless what tomorrow brought, people should know. And jotting down some notes was better than no notes.

So I dragged myself out of bed and picked up where I left off—starting with that little group in Briarwood. And always including those special moments with Yeshua. It had been some time since he last appeared and although his absence was supposed to strengthen me, I have to tell you, I really missed him—like a part of me was missing. In any case, words poured onto the page faster than usual and I had to go down to the front desk and beg for more stationery. I'd barely returned, dumping the stack on the table, when I heard the sound of lapping water. I turned to see it was night and I was back on my beach at Puget Sound.

How I loved this place, its silence and its peace. I watched moonlight sparkle off the incoming water as the tide flowed toward me across the dark sand. I breathed deeply, savoring the smell of salt water, vegetation, and evergreen trees. There were memories here, more than I could count. And they seemed a lifetime ago. In many ways, they were. Another life, another Will Thomas.

I looked down, pleased to see Siggy standing beside me. I gave him a pat. "We've come a long way, haven't we, fella?"

"Yes, you have."

I turned to Yeshua who stood beside me wearing his standard sandals and robe.

"Where have you been?" I asked. It was part accusation and part emotion. And before he could correct my theology, I added, "I know, I know, you're always with me. But still . . ."

He looked down smiling. I sensed a trace of sadness as he finally looked up and motioned for us to walk down the beach. Neither of us spoke, the sand quietly creaking under our feet. I saw movement in the sky and looked up to see a giant bird circling high overhead. "What on earth? Eagles don't fly this time of—" I caught myself, the answer already dawning. "That's no eagle, is it?"

Another gentle smile. "He's always with you too."

"Why isn't he down here with us?"

"He's your power source, Will, not your friend. And tonight . . ." his voice softened, "tonight this is between friends."

I turned to see his eyes shiny with moisture. "It's about tomorrow, isn't it," I said.

"Yes."

"What's going to happen?"

"That's up to you."

"Free will?"

"Always."

"But you know what I'll choose."

"Always."

We continued to walk, the silence returning. My mind drifted to Patricia's admonition to pray, and then to last night's gathering on the hotel roof. Finally, I spoke, "They think, that prayer group on the rooftop, they think I'm some sort of angel, a 'messenger.'"

"They're a perceptive bunch."

"So, declaring the drought, that wasn't enough? I'm supposed to give some sort of message?"

"Only if you want."

"But . . ." I paused, then shook my head.

"What, Will?"

I frowned, struggling to define the thoughts that had formed and congealed over the past several hours of writing; not only about my time in the desert but about the many, many months since we first met. "What if . . ." I hesitated. "What if I'm through wanting what I want?" My frown deepened. I tried again. "What if I just want what you want?"

He smiled and looked out over the water, then back to me. "It's happened, hasn't it?"

"What do you mean?"

"My will becoming yours." I slowed to a stop. He continued, "It's no longer my will, is it? Now it's our will. It's no longer how I think, it's how we think."

I took a breath, surprised at how uneven it came. Somewhere in the back of my mind a Scripture bubbled to the surface. "*We have the mind of Christ.*"

He answered quietly, "I promised you from the beginning that it would happen. And not just your mind, Will." It was his turn to quote, "*I will give you a new heart and put a new spirit within you.*"

"It's true, then," my own voice grew softer. "The transformation you always talked about."

He nodded. "*I pray . . . that all of them may be one, Father, just as you are in me, and I am in you. May they also be in us.*"

"That was your prayer."

"It's always been my prayer."

I stood in silence trying to absorb it all. "And so tomorrow is . . ."

"Your choice."

I started to nod, then stopped and shook my head. "No," I said. "It's our choice. Yours and mine." With a touch of whimsy, I added, "Whether I understand it or not."

He turned to me, eyes filling with moisture. "Yes, my friend. "It is ours."

I stared down at the sand. "Could you . . ." I swallowed. "Could you show me? Just a little . . . so I'll know what to expect?"

He said nothing, as if trying to decide, then suddenly we stood in bright sunlight atop the steps of the Lincoln Memorial. Below us, stretching along both sides of the reflecting pool, was a massive crowd. They were agitated, but they were listening—to me. The future me standing at a plexiglass lectern reading from the Bible.

I turned to Yeshua, my panic rising, "There must be a hundred thousand people here."

"Or more."

"But—"

"Shh." He motioned back to the other me. "Listen."

"*I know your deeds,*" I was reading, "*that you are neither cold nor hot; I wish that you were cold or hot.*'"

I spun back to Yeshua. "I can't do that. I love you, but . . . I can't."

He smiled. "Of course you can't."

"Then . . .?"

He motioned toward the sky where the bird I'd seen earlier, and so many times before, was circling. Only now he was a thousand times bigger with white, translucent wings hovering over the entire National Mall.

"He'll protect me?" I asked.

"He'll empower you."

"There's a difference?"

He gently placed a hand on my shoulder. I turned and saw the most amazing look of tenderness in his eyes.

Immediately we stood in the midst of a screaming mob. I looked down and saw the other me lying at our feet. My head was wet with blood. And holding it in her lap was . . . Darlene Pratford.

"Hang in there!" she cried. "Don't wuss out on me now, Will Thomas! Hang in there!"

The other me looked up to her, smiling, trying to speak. She leaned closer, putting her ear to my lips. Then she pulled back, shaking her head, "No! Not me! No, I can't!"

Again, I tried to speak, blood burbling from my mouth. "Chip," I coughed. "He'll help."

The scene should have been terrifying. But it wasn't. Instead, as I watched, I felt a calmness creeping over me. A quiet certainty.

Suddenly we were back in the hotel room; the noise of the crowd replaced by Chip's snoring. As the vision cleared, I turned to Yeshua and asked, "That's what will happen tomorrow?"

"If you choose."

"It's what we want?" I asked, more statement than question.

He nodded.

I took a slow breath. "It won't be easy, will it?"

"I didn't come to make life easy, Will. I came to make men great."

"Will it do any good?"

"Your children will bless you forever."

"I . . . don't have children."

He gave another smile and suddenly we stood in a lush, green meadow, surrounded by thousands upon thousands of people, every age, every race. And they were all laughing and waving to us—to me.

I shouted to Yeshua over the crowd. "I don't understand! Are these people—"

"Your children, Will. From our union. Yours and mine."

The scene vanished as quickly as it appeared. I closed my eyes, trying to understand. "And this is all from . . . ?"

"Our union."

I opened them. "And it begins tomorrow?"

"For those who have ears to hear."

"But . . ." I scowled. "If I'm gone, how will they hear?"

He nodded to the papers on my table, then over to Chip. The kid's mouth ajar, slightly drooling.

"You're kidding me."

"What did Patricia say? 'I have a weakness for jackasses'?"

I shook my head, marveling—and knowing the reference wasn't limited to Chip.

"Alright," I said. "I understand. But shouldn't I prepare? What should I do in the meantime?"

"Abide. I'll give you the words when you need them. Until then, simply abide."

"Like in Vegas."

"Like in Vegas. You might also want to read up on my letters, the ones I dictated to my churches."

"In Revelation?"

"Particularly Laodicea."

"That's what I was reading to the crowd."

"Yes."

"If I remember, you were pretty tough on that church."

He took a deep breath then quietly repeated a phrase I'd heard from him only once before: "Severe mercy."

Silence crept over our conversation. I remained quiet, a type of reverence, until I had to ask, "And after that? After I study those letters, then what? The rally isn't until late afternoon. I still have plenty of time to fret and worry."

"But you aren't, are you?"

"Fretting and worrying?"

He simply smiled.

I frowned, then shook my head. "How weird. With everything you just showed me, why aren't I afraid?"

"Why should you be?"

I paused but already knew the answer. "Because you'll be there?"

"We'll all be there."

I nodded as another thought came to mind. "And because . . ." He waited for me to finish, "Because it is our will."

There was no missing the pride spreading across his face.

"But I should do something," I said. "Between now and then."

"You could always finish your book."

I glanced at the papers on the table. "It's hardly a book."

"Give me what you have, Will. I'll take care of the rest."

I nodded. Then, blowing out my breath, I reached down and pulled out the chair. When I looked back, Yeshua was gone. No surprise. I took a seat, sat a long moment digesting all I'd seen and heard. I glanced over to the radio alarm. I'd missed taking Patricia to the airport and my heart sank, but only a little. There were other issues. After reading and re-reading his letter to Laodicea a half dozen times, I picked up the hotel pen and returned to writing.

Hours later, after Chip put down a hearty breakfast (or two) and I told him my decision, he did his best to dissuade me. "You know what Proctor's about," he argued. "You know how evil he is. Why are you letting him use you?"

I tried to explain Proctor wasn't using me, but I was using him. Of course, Chip didn't buy it and I didn't blame him. He wasn't used to Yeshua's upside-down logic, let alone his martial arts skill of using the enemy's own power to destroy itself. He had no idea. Not yet.

Eventually, he called Trevor and the die was cast.

Hours flew and, thanks to a couple pitchers of hotel coffee, I was writing up a storm. It was close to five o'clock when Chip finally interrupted. "Well dude, if we're going to go, we might as well get it over with."

I looked up surprised. "You're coming with me?"

"Of course." Then, seeing my expression, he demanded, "What are you smiling about?"

I simply shook my head. I glanced down to Siggy who chose to spend the entire afternoon at my feet. "You'll keep an eye on the pup?" I asked.

"Of course."

I reached down and patted Siggy. "Good boy, good boy. You're the best, aren't you." He looked up at me, thumping his tail and softly whining. It was almost like he understood. Given all we'd been through, maybe he did.

I stared at the papers before me, then finished the last sentence. When it was complete, I paused, looked over the work . . . and laid down my pen for the final time.

CHAPTER
TWENTY-NINE

I GOTTA TELL you, Uncle Will was fantastic. 'Cause way back in Vegas when he prayed at Trevor's convention, it was like a major train wreck. That's why I told him to skip the rally. Well, that and 'cause Proctor is like some sort of anti-Christ. Anyway, there were thousands of people at the Mall. I mean thousands. Pros and cons. Talk about a tinder keg ready to go off. More like a nuclear bomb. I gotta hand it to the cops and National Guard, they did a pretty good job keeping everyone separate with barriers and stuff so they wouldn't kill each other. Proctor haters on the right of the reflecting pool, Proctor fans on the left. Even though the steps leading up to Proctor and the others stunk like sulfur, I was still mad I couldn't stand up there with Will and the other hotshots.

But then I got the call from Amber. They just arrived and parked their RV close—if you call G Street close—so me and Siggy booked it out of there as fast as we could. I started on the right side of the pool, pushing my way through, and I gotta tell you, I never saw so many people ready for a fight. And tons of signs. Things like:

Freedom from Religion!
To hell with your heaven!
Your superstition, NOT mine!

And plenty of shouting. Things hadn't even started and they were chanting: "No ayatollahs, no! No ayatollahs, no!" which, you got to admit, was kind of a mouthful.

Things were happier on the other side, but there was still plenty of shouting: "God's country, not Satan's!" "Devil, go home!" and "Sinners, move to California!"

When I finally got to Amber and the RV, I was sweating pretty good. But it didn't stop us from loving on each other. Boy, I missed that girl. When we came up for air, I saw Fern, Sophia, and Victoria step from the van. Darlene followed with Billie-Jean in her arms.

"Where's Will?" Darlene shouted.

"On stage with Proctor and the big fish," I said.

"Let's go." Amber started pulling me forward. "I wanna see."

"I don't think so, babe."

"What? Why not?"

"A: They won't let you near him. B: It's way too hairy. It's safer if you and Billie-Jean hang here."

She didn't like the idea but agreed.

Not Darlene. "I'm going," she said. "Stay here with the others, but I'm going!" She handed Billie-Jean off to Amber and away she went. Of course, I was torn. I mean I wanted to be with Will, but there was Amber and the baby and—

"Go ahead," Amber ordered.

I turned to her. "What?"

"We'll be fine. Go ahead. He needs you."

I couldn't help smiling. The kid was really growing up. I gave Billie-Jean a quick kiss, and a longer one to Amber before she pushed me away. "Go, go. We're good," she said. "Go!"

I headed back. Funny, in the few minutes I was away, the crowd had gotten bigger and madder. I started from the left side, when some woman standing up on stage kicked things off with "The Star-Spangled Banner." For the moment everyone settled down and joined in, real loud like it was some sort of competition, their voices echoing back and forth across the Mall.

When it was over, some guy led us in the Pledge of Allegiance. It was a bit overkill, but I figured Proctor was trying to make a point. Finally, some old duffer gave a prayer, which was long enough to be a sermon, all about life, liberty, and the pursuit of happiness. Then a couple more suits got up and talked. I was almost to the front when it was Uncle Will's turn.

He carried the hotel Bible with him to the podium. Once he adjusted the mic which gave a little feedback, he began: "I know . . ." His voice was pretty hoarse and he tried again. "I know there's lots of division here." He nodded to his left, "Believers—" A cheer went up from our side. When it finally died down, along with some chanting, he nodded to the right. "And those who refuse to be told what they should believe." It was their turn to cheer. When they finished, he said, "And I believe," he cleared his throat, "I believe God has a message for you both."

Things got real quiet real soon.

"First to my fellow believers." More cheers which he waited to settle down as he opened his Bible. When they finished, he began to read:

"*The faithful and true Witness, the Origin of creation of God says this: I know your deeds, that you are neither cold nor hot; I wish that you were cold or hot.*" He, hesitated, then continued, "*So because you are lukewarm, and neither hot nor cold, I will vomit you out of My mouth.*"

Talk about silence. Everyone was pretty stunned.

He looked up to us. "I believe, the Lord would say this applies to many of us today."

He waited as the murmurings began, then turned to anger and then to shouting. "That's not for us!" "We're for God!" Pointing across the pool, they yelled things like: "It's them! They're ruining this country! They're mocking Christianity!"

As they shouted, Uncle Will cocked his head to the side like he was listening to something else. Then he spoke. Actually, he had to yell to be heard. "God is not about Christianity! God is about Christ!"

Trevor and Proctor, who sat just behind him and to the left, didn't look too thrilled. In fact, Trevor started to rise 'til Proctor motioned him back down.

And Will just kept going. "The Bible says, 'Be holy, because I am holy!' It's not about having your rights offended. It's about your deeds, your filthy rags that nauseate him!"

That didn't help. "God's on our side!" someone shouted. Others agreed and pretty soon the chant went up: "God's with us! God's with us! God's with us!"

To which Will shouted back, "I tell you the truth, God can raise up these stones to be his children!"

Not helpful. They say hell has no fury like a woman scorned. Wrong. Hell has no fury like religious pride scorned. If it wasn't for the police and their barricades, the crowd would have stormed the stage.

Something behind me caught Will's eye. I turned back to see Victoria making her way through the crowd. She held a handful of balloons floating over her head. I figured they were to encourage him, to let him know she'd arrived with the rest of the group. But they had a different effect.

He obviously saw them 'cause he shouted, "You're like empty balloons! God's commands are good, but you cannot be good by yourself. When you fail, you are full of guilt. When you succeed, you're full of pride," he motioned to the other side, "and full of judgment."

He was definitely losing them. We all knew it. So did he. He closed his eyes, taking a long deep breath, and it was like something coming over him. Then he opened them and shouted:

"Jesus doesn't want your religion! He wants your hearts! Ask him to forgive you, yes! But he must come inside. You cannot be good on your own. He must come inside and grow! You must let him change you from the inside out!"

It sounded like a pretty good sermon, at least to those who weren't shouting and pushing at the barricades. Things were definitely getting crazy up front, and the cops could barely hold them back. But Will, he barely noticed. Instead, he turned to the other side and riled them up:

"And you," he looked down and read. *"You say, 'I am rich, and have become wealthy, and have need of nothing,' and you do not know that you are wretched, miserable, poor, blind, and naked—"*

That pretty much did it. Now both sides were crazy mad. And still he went on. *"I advise you to buy from Me gold refined by fire so that you may become rich, and white garments so that you may clothe yourself and the shame of your nakedness will not be revealed—"*

The roar drowned out the rest. But Uncle Will, being an equal opportunity offender, looked up and continued shouting, "You want freedom, but you are slaves, mastered by your desires! You keep trying to fill your hunger with grosser and grosser immorality—thinking your greater perversions will fill your emptiness!"

That's when the first rock flew—and missed him. He turned back to the Bible and read some more: *"Those whom I love I rebuke and discipline; Therefore be zealous and repent. Behold, I stand at the door and knock; if anyone hears My voice and opens the door, I will come into—"*

The second rock missed. The third struck him squarely in the face. That's when the barricades gave way and the people broke through. Police clubs swung but they weren't much help.

"Will!" I pushed and shoved trying to get to him. "Uncle Will!" But there was no way.

Handfuls from both sides swarmed in—swinging fists and placards, even an American flag, its pole hitting Will and knocking him to the ground. Eventually the cops got in there and pulled them away. I caught a glimpse of Darlene. She'd made it through the chaos and was up onto the stage kneeling next to him.

A tear gas canister landed near me. It spun, spewing smoke, burning my throat and eyes. I coughed and spit, almost gagging. And then I saw it. Maybe it was my imagination, maybe from blurry eyes. But when I looked up, I saw a light hovering over us. Over the whole Mall. It was like a cloud, only blinding bright. And in the center was what looked like a man carved out of the light. I turned to the people around me, but they were too busy coughing and retching and swearing to see. But they did hear it. We all heard it. It was like thunder, exploding all around us. Thunder, but it sounded like words. Maybe it was both. Either way we all froze in our tracks. And the words? There were just five of them:

"Come, enter into my joy!"

By now everybody was looking up, checking the sky. But I seemed to be the only one who saw it. Saw them. Because now there were two in the cloud. The one carved in light and—I don't care what you say, but I know what I saw—beside him was Uncle Will.

EPILOGUE

"SIGGY, GET BACK here. Siggy!" The dog never listens. Instead, he ran off and disappeared around a tower of giant boulders. "Mess around those rocks," I shouted, "and you'll wish you hadn't!"

He didn't care. He just likes to be out and to run, no matter how hot it is. Which is usually why I take these walks before sunrise or after it gets dark. Not that it helps much. Even with Uncle Will's speech and disappearance—which some claim was a kidnapping, others a magic trick—and Proctor winning as president, the drought just keeps going. Then there's this whole locust thing happening in the Midwest. Not that the bugs have much to eat, but whatever is left, is theirs.

"Siggy!" I traipsed toward the rocks. The latest sandstorms, and there were plenty, kept moving stuff around so even the places I knew looked different. Which is okay. The point is, I needed these walks. Especially with all that's coming down. And I'm not talking politics, though there's plenty of that. It's mostly this movement that's picking up speed. People, like those guys praying on the rooftop back in D.C. or, last week, when I Zoomed with Sparky at the prison where Uncle Will used to teach. Everyone says stuff is happening. Even Patricia, down in wherever she's at. She doesn't call it a revival but a reformation. She says, people are "aligning their hearts to God." I suppose that's one way of putting it. However you say it, it's keeping me busy. Here in Briarwood, our group just keeps getting bigger and bigger. People coming in from Vegas and all sorts of places. Some are camping out, some are even moving in—which explains Sophia hustling to get her realtor's license.

And remember Fern? It's even forced her to come out of her shell. Sophia's got her running our "hospitality unit" which helps get the newbies situated. Her pimp even came out to visit, but only once. Some of our bigger members drove him over to the closest ER . . . after they offered their own version of hospitality.

Victoria's also doing her part. She scored some deal with a balloon company and is busy mailing them out to folks all over the country. Funny, seeing everybody with Bibles and balloons. But after Uncle Will's speech in D.C., I hear lots of groups are using them for a symbol. And Darlene? She's spending her time coordinating those groups. Mostly internet stuff—keeping people on the same page while dodging the authorities so she doesn't get shut down. Oh, and Cowboy? He's so deep in politics we hardly ever see him—though there's a rumor he'll soon be running for some sort of office.

"Siggy!" I rounded the last bunch of boulders and saw him digging up a storm. "Come on, fella. What are you doing?" I joined him but he just kept digging. "All right, fine," I said, "suit yourself." I crossed over to a nearby boulder and sat. The sun wasn't up yet, but it was already getting hot.

Like I was saying, I really need these walks. I'm not exactly famous for my humility (something Amber's more than willing to help me with), but for someone my age to talk to all these people about God every Sunday? Don't get me wrong, I've got a pretty good handle on the Bible, but there's still plenty of stuff to learn, even from those old guys like Spurgeon or Wesley or that Thomas à Kempis dude.

Back to me and Amber. We're thinking of getting married. 'Course everyone says we're way too young, but the way things are going I figure this ol' world won't be around much longer so we might as well enjoy the fringe benefits while we can, if you know what I mean. Wink, wink.

Siggy had dug a hole a good two, maybe three feet when he started to whimper. I quickly got up to check. "What's a matter, boy? You get bit?" But he wasn't hurt. He just found something. I kneeled to look. It was wood, an old board. And below it, some cardboard. "Scoot over, fella, let me help."

After digging another foot or so, I got a grip on the cardboard and pulled. It was a bunch of pieces taped together to cover a hole. But it wasn't a hole. Because the more we dug the more it looked like a window. Me and Uncle Will had been out this way a few times looking for his little shack, but everything changed so much we never found it. But this . . .

It was a trick, pulling out the cardboard and keeping back the sand without it all pouring in, but we succeeded. Mostly. And when it was big enough, I dropped my head down and poked it inside. It was definitely a room. Plenty of sand, but definitely a room. I pulled out my phone and shined in the light. There wasn't much to see. A half-buried cot and what looked like a potbelly stove. But just below me, under the window, was a table. It was covered in sand but on top I could make out a big pile of legal pads.

No way was I going inside. But with my great athletic abilities I was able to reach down to one of the pads and pull it out. The page was covered in handwriting. I turned it and there was more. And then another page and another. It looked like Uncle Will's writing, like the papers I kept from D.C.

I looked back at the window. Who knew how many of these were in there. But no way was I crawling in on my own. I'd come back later in the daylight, bring some other folks with me. Until then, I crossed back to my boulder and sat. The sun was just beginning to rise when I started reading. You could tell it was Uncle Will, alright. And he was arguing with someone. Not really arguing, more like having heated discussions. Just Will and some guy with an unusual name. But that's okay, because Uncle Will was kinda unusual too, right? Which, in a strange way, gives me some comfort. 'Cause if God can use someone like Uncle Will, I suppose he can use anybody.

Soli de Gloria

Warrior
Rendezvous with GOD, Volume Six

DISCUSSION QUESTIONS

CHAPTER ONE

Full Disclosure: I have a secluded field in back of the house where no one (including family) can see me. And since there's little on TV these days, I go back there to pray. Often times, I just sit there and quietly adore God. Other times I'll rant and rave at the enemy—sometimes with the soundtrack of *The Gladiator* playing through my headphones (I said, "full disclosure" right?) reminding the "accuser of the brethren" who Christ is and who Christ says I am. Would I do it in public like Will? Never. Do I see angels and demons. Never. But it doesn't stop me.

1. Do you have any unique and personal ways to connect to the Lord?

CHAPTER TWO

1. In the 1500s, St. John of the Cross wrote about something called the Dark Night of the Soul— a time

when we feel abandoned by God, but a time he uses to draw us deeper into his presence. It's like teaching my daughters to walk; I pull back just a foot or two and let them struggle to reach me. Do they feel abandoned? Yes. Then why on earth do I do it? Why does God?

2. Have you witnessed people trying to sell Jesus so badly, they lie about how easy and painless Christianity is? I wonder what they do with all his promises about dying to self, having tribulation in this life, being hated by the world? Or, as he says in Luke 9:23, "Whoever wants to be my disciple must deny themselves and take up their cross daily and follow me." And yet Jesus promises us a peace the world does not understand. How does that paradox work?

3. No shame or blame here, but when Jesus calls us to become Olympian athletes of faith, what excuses do we find to become couch potatoes of leisure?

CHAPTER THREE

1. What is Will's eventual understanding of false humility? Do you agree?

2. How can false humility prevent us from becoming all God designed us to be?

3. What is the difference between false humility and true humility?

CHAPTER FOUR

1. Most of my life I've been underqualified to do what God calls me to do. And yet, somehow, after I've given him all I can, he makes up for my deficiency. Can you think of times he's done that with you?

2. What areas are you still afraid to say yes to because you're sure you don't have enough of what it takes?

CHAPTER FIVE

As a "doer" the concept of being still is difficult for me. Yet when I exercise the discipline of stillness and solitude (and, yes, it's a discipline), the benefits have always been rewarding—seldom at the moment, but always eventually.

1. What areas do you find it difficult to be still and know he is God?

2. What can you do to be more successful in this endeavor?

CHAPTER SIX

1. What did the Trappist monk mean in writing, "Go into the desert not to escape other men but in order to find them in God?"

2. Not everyone can go into the desert. What are other ways of detoxifying our souls to better appreciate God and his children?

CHAPTER SEVEN

Dreams are fascinating. And we certainly see them in Scripture—from Joseph in the Old Testament to Joseph in the New. Of course, not every dream is from God but over the years I can think of a few that helped direct my life, one time even saving it. Here's an interesting quote from Job 33:14–16: "For God does speak—now one way, now another—though no one perceives it. In a dream, in a vision of the night, when deep sleep falls on people as they slumber in their beds he may speak in their ears and terrify them with warnings."

1. Are there times you feel God has directed you through dreams?

CHAPTER NINE

1. In regards to the cycle of being loved and returning love, of giving and receiving, I play a game with God. It's called: Who Can Outgive Who? And I always lose. It seems no matter how hard I try, he just doesn't have the knack for losing. What are some ways you've seen him win in your life?

Will is about to experience the importance of community. As a closet introvert, it is so easy for me to drop into the mentality of, "It's just you and me, right, God?" But what a loss. By only looking into the mirror, I deprive myself of all the wonderful diversity of others around me. If we're called the body of Christ and I'm, say, the left little toe, what a shame to believe his whole body is nothing but a left little toe.

Being "spurred" is not a comfortable feeling but in Hebrews 10:24–25 we read: "And let us consider how we may spur one another on toward love and good deeds, not giving up meeting together, as some are in the habit of doing, but encouraging one another—and all the more as you see the Day approaching."

2. What are some practical steps to take to prevent becoming a solo Christian?

CHAPTER TEN

As I've mentioned, the following three verses are pillars to my walk with Christ. When combined, the effects have been life-changing.

> *"And we know that in all things God works for the good of those who love him, who have been called according to his purpose."* Romans 8:28

> *"Consider it pure joy, my brothers and sisters, whenever you face trials of many kinds, because you know that the testing of your faith produces perseverance. Let perseverance finish its work so that you may be mature and complete, not lacking anything."* James 1:2–4

> *"Rejoice always, pray continually, give thanks in all circumstances; for this is God's will for you in Christ Jesus."* 1 Thessalonians 5:16–18

1. If you really believed these verses, I mean REALLY BELIEVED them, how would they change your life?

CHAPTER ELEVEN

I think one of the most autobiographical things in this series is how God always gives Will the opportunity to step into what Will is sure to be an impossible situation. Because I made this crazy promise as an eighteen-year-old to always say yes to God (regardless of how unqualified I was), he keeps taking me up on my promise. Whether it's becoming a film writer/director (when I'd seen only three movies in my life before college), or an award-winning author of dozens of books (when I'd only read three for recreation before college—if you count *The Cat in the Hat*), or a Bible instructor with no training but a BA in theater arts. In every case he gives me the opportunity to say no—but whenever I say yes, I'm in for an adventure.

1. Are there any areas God is pressing upon you to say yes?

2. Does the saying, "An excuse is a lie wrapped in reason" have any relevancy to your choices?

CHAPTER TWELVE

Another thing about community: Like rocks in a tumbler, the members are often polished into beauty by slamming into each other.

1. God always gives us the choice, but what would happen if we reached out to that annoying person we try to avoid? How could it change them? How could it change us?

CHAPTER THIRTEEN

Fast-growing weeds versus slow-growing oaks. I'm often frustrated with God for taking his sweet time on issues. But when I look back, the quick fixes are often momentary compared to the success of his slow and steady faithfulness.

1. In what areas are you frustrated with God's slower timetable? What advantages can you see if he take his time?

CHAPTER FOURTEEN

1. Jesus calls us to die to ourselves and come alive in him. In what ways do we try to fool ourselves that our flesh is dead?

2. Do you agree that the flesh will do anything to keep living, even become religious? Any examples come to mind?

CHAPTER FIFTEEN

1. Pastors are my heroes. Not the bossy and manipulative ones or the ones who pastor to avoid getting their hands dirty with the world—but the ones who

seriously lay down their lives for their flock. It's often a lonely, thankless job. What pastors like that have impacted your life?

2. What do you think about dropping them a card of thanks or inviting them to dinner?

3. Back to the balloon analogy (the theme of this series): behavior modification versus spiritual transformation. Does that exclude responsibility on our part? If not, where do we fit in the equation?

CHAPTER SIXTEEN

1. If a devout Christian is called to be a politician, what are the dangers?

2. Like Fern, there are so many ways we insulate ourselves from being re-hurt. Sadly, this can shield us from the very healing we need. What was behind the action that momentarily broke through Fern's insulation? How can we apply that to ourselves or to those who have suffered in the past?

CHAPTER SEVENTEEN

1. How is Harry's story applicable to Christ's teaching about our own lives?

CHAPTER NINETEEN

1. Is Will being unreasonable by refusing to speak with Proctor and Trevor?

2. Some think it's simplistic to say we can make the right decision by simply abiding in Christ? What is your opinion?

CHAPTER TWENTY

1. What are the advantages of a large, successful church? What are the disadvantages?

2. Instead of church multiplication, what would you say are the three top issues leading to church division?

3. What guard rails and safety nets should be in place to encourage diversity but not division?

CHAPTER TWENTY-ONE

1. What is your opinion about the three lights method of finding God's will?

2. When does it work?

3. When does it fail?

CHAPTER TWENTY-TWO

I'm always startled to see seeds I planted long ago and forgotten begin to grow.

1. Can you think of a time when an unlikely encounter of yours turned a life to Christ?

2. I think God likes a good challenge. Why not choose an "impossible case" and bear down in prayer to prove him?

CHAPTER TWENTY-THREE

1. Is God's wrath an extension of his love? How?

2. At this writing the term "woke" is being thrown around like a Frisbee. It has different meanings for different people. In your opinion what if any are the negative elements of the meaning?

3. What if any are the positive?

CHAPTER TWENTY-FOUR

1. In forcing God to show his hand, Will plays "Bible roulette." How is that a good idea? How is it bad?

2. My prophetic friends have described the smell of sulfur (brimstone) when they're in the presence of evil, and the smell of flowers when in the presence of the Lord. For those of us unable to physically experience God, what are some other ways we can encounter him?

CHAPTER TWENTY-FIVE

1. If God honors our free will by laying out a banquet for us to eat or refuse, to what extent should we reward or penalize those who exercise their free will?

2. What is your opinion of John Calvin's laws in sixteenth-century Geneva calling for fines and imprisonment of those who did not attend church regularly? Or the Spanish Inquisition calling for prison, torture and/or death for those who did not adhere to Catholic orthodoxy?

3. Where is the balance? How can we ensure our free will to partake of God's goodness and not threaten those who choose to ignore it?

CHAPTER TWENTY-SIX

For years I had a cartoon above my desk of a huge monster looming over and ready to destroy a little boy. The child is motioning over his shoulder to a giant pair of sandaled feet and legs so tall they stretch out of the frame. In the caption, the boy simply says: "I'm with him."

I love the thought that despite impossible odds, God and I make up the majority.

CHAPTER TWENTY-SEVEN

1. What are your thoughts about our culture inoculating people with an incomplete or altered gospel to prevent them from catching the real thing?

2. In what ways have we preached an easy faith and a wishy-washy gospel? Has it backfired on us?

3. In what ways have some preached the opposite, and how has that backfired?

4. What is the balance?

CHAPTER TWENTY-EIGHT

1. In Revelation 1:16, John sees the tongue in Jesus's mouth as a two-edged sword. Why two edges and not one?

2. Why is Will, who started out back in Volume One as a skeptic and a bit of a coward, now unafraid of what he's about to encounter?

3. In what ways has Will's mind been transformed to Christ's? In what ways has the Holy Spirit changed his heart of stone into a heart of flesh?

4. In what specific ways have you been transformed?

5. In what specific ways would you like to be transformed?

CHAPTER TWENTY-NINE

1. In what areas would the letter to Laodicea apply to the Western church?

2. If God is love, why does he threaten to vomit his church out of his mouth?

EPILOGUE

And so we come to the end of Will's journey as he goes from:

> *Rendezvous with God*: Volume One - Skeptic to believer.
>
> *Temptation*: Volume Two - Discovering our identity in Christ, not what others think.
>
> *Commune*: Volume Three - Examining Jesus's version of prayer.
>
> *Insight*: Volume Four - Turning faith into action.
>
> *Seer*: Volume Five - Discerning and challenging false teaching.
>
> *Warrior*: Volume Six - Becoming the person Christ has called us to be.

In this series I tried a new form of writing. Instead of praying and then going to work, I prayed as I worked. I'd purposefully write Will into a corner, then turn to the chair I pretend Jesus sits in when I'm writing and say, "Now what?" The answers that bubbled up in my brain were often as surprising to me as they may have been to readers.

In any case, thanks for taking this journey with me. I hope at times you found it as edifying in the reading as I did in the writing. May the Lord continue transforming your mind and your heart into his.

Previous Praise for Bill Myers's Novels

Blood of Heaven

"With the chill of a Robin Cooke techno-thriller and the spiritual depth of a C. S. Lewis allegory, this book is a fast-paced, action-packed thriller." —Angela Hunt, *NY Times* best-selling author

"Enjoyable and provocative. I wish I'd thought of it!" —Frank E. Peretti, *This Present Darkness*

Eli

"The always surprising Myers has written another clever and provocative tale." —Booklist

"With this thrilling and ominous tale, Myers continues to shine brightly in speculative fiction based upon biblical truth. Highly recommended." —*Library Journal*

"Myers weaves a deft, affecting tale." —*Publishers Weekly* The Face of God

"Strong writing, edgy . . . replete with action . . ." —*Publishers Weekly*

Fire of Heaven

"I couldn't put the *Fire of Heaven* down. Bill Myers's writing is crisp, fast-paced, provocative . . . A very compelling story." —Francine Rivers, *NY Times* best-selling author

Soul Tracker

"*Soul Tracker* provides a treat for previous fans of the author but also a fitting introduction to those unfamiliar with his work. I'd recommend the book to anyone, initiated or not. But be careful to check your expectations at the door . . . it's not what you think it is." —Brian Reaves, *Fuse* magazine

"Thought provoking and touching, this imaginative tale blends elements of science fiction with Christian theology." —*Library Journal*

"Myers strikes deep into the heart of eternal truth with this imaginative first book of the Soul Tracker series. Readers will be eager for more." —*Romantic Times* magazine

Angel of Wrath

"Bill Myers is a genius." —Lee Stanley, producer, Gridiron Gang

Saving Alpha

"When one of the most creative minds I know gets the best idea he's ever had and turns it into a novel, it's fasten-your-seat-belt time. This one will be talked about for a long time." —Jerry B. Jenkins, author of *Left Behind*

"An original masterpiece." —Dr. Kevin Leman, best-selling author

"If you enjoy white-knuckle, page-turning suspense, with a brilliant blend of cutting-edge apologetics, Saving Alpha will grab you for a long, long time." —Beverly Lewis, *NY Times* best-selling author

"I've never seen a more powerful and timely illustration of the incarnation. Bill Myers has a way of making the gospel accessible and relevant to readers of all ages. I highly recommend this book." —Terri Blackstock, *NY Times* best-selling author

"A brilliant novel that feeds the mind and heart, Saving Alpha belongs at the top of your reading list." —Angela Hunt, *NY Times* best-selling author

"Saving Alpha is a rare combination that is both entertaining and spiritually provocative. It has a message of deep spiritual significance that is highly relevant for these times." —Paul Cedar, Chairman, Mission America Coalition

"Once again Myers takes us into imaginative and intriguing depths, making us feel, think and ponder all at the same time. Relevant and entertaining. Saving Alpha is not to be missed." —James Scott Bell, best-selling author

The Voice

"A crisp, express-train read featuring 3D characters, cinematic settings and action, and, as usual, a premise I wish I'd thought of. Succeeds splendidly! Two thumbs up!" —Frank E. Peretti, *This Present Darkness*

"Nonstop action and a brilliantly crafted young heroine will keep readers engaged as this adventure spins to its thought-provoking conclusion. This book explores the intriguing concept of God's power as not only the creator of the universe, but as its very essence." —Kris Wilson, *CBA* magazine

"It's a real 'what if ?' book with plenty of thrills . . . that will definitely create questions all the way to its thought-provoking finale. The success of Myers's stories is a sweet combination of a believable storyline, intense action, and brilliantly crafted, yet flawed characters." —Dale Lewis, TitleTrakk.com

The Seeing

"Compels the reader to burn through the pages. Cliff-hangers abound, and the stakes are raised higher and higher as the story progresses—intense, action-shocking twists!" —Title Trakk.com

When the Last Leaf Falls

"A wonderful novella . . . Any parent will warm to the humorous reminiscences and the loving exasperation of this father for his strong-willed daughter . . . Compelling characters and fresh, vibrant anecdotes of one family's faith journey." —*Publishers Weekly*

Rendezvous with God

"Gritty. Unflinching. In your face. Emotionally wrenching. *Rendezvous with God* is Bill Myers at the top of his imaginative game. A rip-roaring read you can neither tear yourself away from, nor dare experience without thinking." —Jerry Jenkins, *New York Times*-bestselling novelist and author of the Left Behind series

"A teacher and a storyteller, Bill Myers welcomes, disarms, then edifies in this tight and seamless weave of story and truth. It's innovative, 'outside the box,' but that's why it works so well, bringing the reader profound and practical wisdom, the heart of Jesus, in modern, Everyman terms—and always with the quick-draw Myers wit. Jesus talked to me through this book. I was blessed, and from some of my inner shadows, set free. Follow along. Let it minister." —Frank Peretti, *New York Times*-bestselling author of *This Present Darkness*, *The Visitation*, and *Illusion*

"If you have ever wished for a personal encounter with Jesus Christ, *Rendezvous with God* may be the next best thing. Bringing Jesus into contemporary times, Bill Myers shows us what Jesus came to do, and why He had to do it. This little book packs a powerful punch." —Angela Hunt, *New York Times*-bestselling author of *The Jerusalem Road* series

BILL MYERS

Seer

a novel

Rendezvous with God Volume Five

9781956454574 – $18.00
eBook 9781956454581 – $9.99

Insight
9781956454420 – $18

eBook 9781956454437 – $12.99

BILL MYERS

a novel

Insight

Rendezvous with God Volume Four

Commune
9781956454246 – $17
eBook 9781956454253 – $9.99

BILL
MYERS

a novel

Commune

Rendezvous with God Volume Three

Temptation
9781956454024 – $16

eBook 9781956454031 – $9.99

BILL
MYERS

a novel

Temptation

Rendezvous with God Volume Two

Rendezvous with God
9781735428581 – $16

eBook 9781735428598 – $.99

BILL MYERS

Rendezvous with GOD

a novel